Daughters of Muscadine

DAUGHTERS of MUSCADINE

stories

Monic Ductan

Published by Fireside Industries Books
An imprint of The University Press of Kentucky

Editorial and Sales Offices: The University Press of Kentucky
663 South Limestone Street, Lexington, Kentucky 40508-4008
www.kentuckypress.com

Library of Congress Cataloging-in-Publication Data

Names: Ductan, Monic, author.
Title: Daughters of Muscadine : stories / Monic Ductan.
Description: Lexington, Kentucky : Fireside Industries, [2023]
Identifiers: LCCN 2023007284 | ISBN 9781950564330 (hardcover ; acid-free paper) | ISBN 9781950564347 (pdf) | ISBN 9781950564354 (epub)
Subjects: LCSH: Women, Black—Fiction. | Women—Appalachian Region, Southern—Fiction. | Women—Georgia—Fiction. | Appalachian Region, Southern—Fiction. | Georgia—Fiction. | LCGFT: Short stories.
Classification: LCC PS3604.U356 D38 2023 | DDC 813/.6—dc23/eng/20230421
LC record available at https://lccn.loc.gov/2023007284

This book is printed on acid-free paper meeting the requirements of the American National Standard for Permanence in Paper for Printed Library Materials.

Manufactured in the United States of America

For Black women, wherever you are in this world.

Contents

Black Water

In Muscadine, there's a legend about my great-grandmother, Ida Pearl Crawley, who was lynched for killing a white family, the Munsons. This was back in 1920, and Pearl had a little shack on Herbert Munson's farm and worked as his cook. Pearl had been doing it with Munson for God knows how long. He'd given her two kids, and she wanted him to deed her a piece of land on the farm, but Herbert Munson said no, so Pearl torched his house, killing Herbert and most of his family. Only two of the Munson kids survived the fire. As for Pearl, she made it halfway to Atlanta before they caught her. They got her back to Munson Plantation and hung her from an oak overlooking the charred plantation house.

Here in Muscadine, talk of Pearl is still plentiful as the mosquitoes that swirl around Harmony Shoals.

"They say Pearl comes out in the evening, just before dark," Daddy said, taking his eyes off the road. He looked over his shoulder at my sister, Kiki, in the back seat of our Ford Granada. It was just the three of us. Mama had left again, was staying with her sister since she and Daddy were fighting.

"Pearl, she comes out of the shoals. It's where she was born. I saw her there one time, standing over a fire, holding a chicken up by its feet," Daddy said.

I looked into the back seat to see that Kiki's face was all chewed up in a frown as she pulled at the hem of her yellow sundress. Kiki was only six, and anytime Daddy told us a scary story, she had trouble sleeping that night.

"You know we come from Pearl, son?"

I rolled my eyes. I was twelve years old then, and I had heard Daddy, more than once, brag about being the grandson of Herbert Munson. But I had gone to school with the Munsons since kindergarten, and not one of them claimed me. One time in third grade, Phillip Munson tossed his blue crayon down and said to me, "We ain't no kin. Look at yo' skin. It's black as I don't know *what.*"

Far as I was concerned, I hated the Munson boys, and I hated our charcoaled great-granddaddy Herbert. But it was Pearl people still talked about; at least that was good for something.

Daddy's foot mashed down on the gas, revving the Ford's engine. The car's entire body shook. My teeth rattled together. I held a deck of cards in my hands. I'd been practicing a card trick that I wanted to try on my cousin Pie Face. It was Labor Day, and we were headed to Uncle Lester's house to cook out.

"Boo!" Daddy yelled suddenly, turning toward Kiki in the back seat.

I jumped, dropping the cards all over my lap and the floorboard of the Granada. Kiki screamed. The little beads on the ends of her plaits clicked together as she stretched out across the back seat and buried her head underneath her arms.

Daddy laughed like it was going out of style, slapped his hand on the steering wheel. Daddy was so light-skinned I could see the blue veins crisscrossing his arms. He had a beer gut, but other than that, he was skinny, maybe a little too skinny in the legs.

I let out a frustrated sigh as I leaned over to pick up the cards I'd dropped.

"No harm done, Pritch," Daddy said.

Daddy and I were both named Pritchard. When I was little everyone called me Little Pritchard, which I hated. I liked being called Pritch better, but one time at the park a bunch of bullies started calling me bitch instead of Pritch. Daddy had overheard them and yelled at me for not standing up for myself. I knew Daddy thought of me as a little runt. Here I was going on thirteen and not even five foot tall yet. I kept hoping I'd shoot up to six foot four; that way I'd be an inch taller than Daddy.

When we turned into Uncle Lester's driveway, Daddy had to slow us down because of all the ruts and bumps. Our pace gave me a chance to study the house and yard as we got closer. Even though it wasn't pretty to look at, I loved my uncle's house because it was always peaceful and the adults never fought like my parents did. Made shotgun-style, the house was covered in forest-green paint and had teal-green shutters. The front windows opened out instead of up, and a dog always sat in the yard. Back then the dog was Murray, the ugliest basset hound you ever saw. That day, he lay under a moss-covered tree. His ears drooped; even his eyelids were droopy and half-shut, as though he couldn't be bothered to keep them open.

Uncle Lester and his wife, Aunt Eliza, stood together in front of their grill. I stuck my nose out the window and got a whiff of the charred meat they cooked. Uncle Lester closed the lid of the grill, and smoke moved lazily up toward his beard.

We got out of the car and I helped Kiki tote the things we had brought with us: potato salad, a case of Coke, rolls, and paper towels.

"Lester, brother man, what's happening?" Daddy said, hugging Uncle Lester and clapping him on the back.

Uncle Lester was tall as Daddy, but not nearly as broad-shouldered or imposing. He wore a full beard, even in summer, and his T-shirts always stretched tight over his round belly.

Eliza wore a pink tank top and flowered Bermuda shorts. Her pink makeup had melted against her skin. Eliza came forward and hugged Kiki and me. Daddy mashed his lips against her brown-and-pink cheek and made a wet, smooching sound.

It always disgusted me how Daddy flirted with women. Every checker at the grocery store in town got a smile and a wink. I wondered if they thought Daddy was handsome.

Pie Face came out of the house, banged the screen door shut, and jumped over the porch railing. He landed on his feet but in a crouch, his arms out in front, his butt only inches from the ground. Kiki and me busted up laughing.

"You got that table set, boy?" Uncle Lester asked.

"Everything's ready," Pie Face said as he came over to me and punched my arm lightly.

It was the 1990s, and Pie Face had that high-top fade that was so popular with Black boys back then. Though only two years older than me, Pie Face was nearly as tall as Daddy and Uncle Lester. It just wasn't fair that he was fourteen and already six foot tall. I prayed I'd hit a growth spurt soon.

Us kids went into the house behind Aunt Eliza.

Granddaddy Crawley looked up from the TV and nodded at us. His name was Milton Crawley, and he was the son of Ida Pearl and Herbert Munson. Granddaddy was little bitty when his parents died, so he was unable to remember them. What he did remember was the Great Depression, and he forever talked about it, telling everyone who would listen that he had picked two hundred pounds of cotton a day each season and drove a model-T Ford. As far as I could see, Granddaddy Crawley had two talents: he could tell funny stories about animals, and he was the best checker player in our family (which says a lot, because every one of us was ace at checkers).

Granddaddy had been old my whole life, but that day he *looked* old. He wasn't wearing his teeth, and the way his flesh caved in over his cheekbones made him look like a skeleton.

I followed Pie Face into the kitchen, where Kiki began to help Aunt Eliza put out the bowls of potato salad and corn on the cob.

The kitchen window was propped open with a tree branch, and a layer of dust and pollen was caked on the window screen.

I sat down at the table across from Pie Face, and as we waited for our daddies to come inside with the meat, I had Pie Face pick a card.

I glanced up at Kiki, who stood behind Pie Face. She put three fingers real casual-like against her forehead. Then, she tugged on her right earlobe, signaling me.

"Is it a three of hearts?" I asked Pie Face.

"Hey! How'd you know that?" he asked.

"Magic."

After dinner, us kids were supposed to go wash the dinner dishes. We took the dishes to the sink, where I licked the barbecue sauce from them and Pie Face put them back in the cupboard.

"Let's go play ball," Pie Face said to me as he pointed out the kitchen window.

I looked out into the backyard to see that Daddy and Uncle Lester were throwing a baseball around while Granddaddy Crawley sat under a shady tree and watched. I didn't really want to play, but my only other choice was to stay inside with Kiki, who was sleepy and kept whining about everything.

I followed Pie Face out to the backyard.

Lester caught with a glove, but Daddy caught each ball barehanded and with *only* one hand. His other hand held a beer. Daddy kept egging Uncle Lester to throw his pitches harder. Each time Lester put a little more heat behind his throw, it pleased Daddy something awful to catch that ball. He never missed. Pie Face and I watched as Daddy caught ball after ball, barely even wincing as each one smacked his bare hand.

"Count me in," Pie Face said, going over to them. He clapped his hands and leaned toward Daddy. Daddy threw him the ball, and Pie Face caught it easily. He was a natural at baseball, had played through middle school and would be going out for the high school team soon.

"Come on, Pritch," Pie Face said. "You in?"

Without waiting for my answer, Pie Face tossed the ball underhanded at me. I almost caught it, but it slipped through my hands, bounced off my sneaker and rolled down the hill toward the high grass. I was too awkward to catch, shoot, rebound, and pretty much do anything athletic.

We tossed the ball in a circle. Daddy threw to Lester, then Lester threw to Pie Face, and Pie Face tossed it underhanded at me. I was the only one who got the underhanded toss, and I still couldn't catch it. Every time I tried, I kept seeing the ball slip through my fingers or picturing how Daddy always held his lips all squeezed together when we played sports.

What'd I ever do to get a screwup like Pritch for a kid? Damn butterfingers. That's what Daddy was probably thinking.

After I dropped the fourth or fifth ball in a row, Daddy sighed and went over to the cooler. As I bent to pick up the ball, I heard him pop the tab on another can of beer. He drank it down in a few gulps, then held up his hand for me to throw him the ball. "Put some heat behind it, boy," he said. I tried to remember how pitchers did it on TV. I hiked up my leg and almost tipped over as I released the ball. It flew wide and barely missed hitting Granddaddy's cane.

"Goddamn it, boy!" Daddy said. "You can't throw straight? Either throw it *to me* or go play dolls with your sister." He punctuated his last sentence with a loud burp. Then, instead of going after the ball, he fished through the ice for another beer. I ran over and picked up the ball. Daddy held up his hand for another throw. Because he was standing so far away, I took a big step toward him.

"No, no, *no,*" Daddy said. "Stay where you are. See can you throw it from there," he said, smirking. "Come on, son. Put some heat on it." He tilted the beer can up and drank from it as he watched me. With beer dribbling off his chin, he said, "And don't do that little sissy wind-up shit neither."

I reared my arm back and hurled it as hard as I could, aiming for Daddy's stomach. But the ball dropped three feet in front of him in the grass. He started laughing so hard he shook. Beer sloshed up and wet his shirt and hand.

I went over to the other side of the yard and sprawled out in the grass by a clump of honeysuckle vines. Murray lay in the grass in front of me. He rolled onto his back, and I rubbed the soft fur on his belly.

A minute later, I looked up to see Granddaddy coming toward me, dragging his ladder-backed chair behind him.

I gave him a mean look.

"Don't worry," Granddaddy said. "I won't tell nobody I seen you crying."

"I ain't crying," I said, wiping a tear from my cheek. "I'm *mad.*"

He sat down in the chair and took a deck of cards from the front pocket of his bib-alls. He asked me to show him the card trick I'd pulled on Pie Face, and I almost started to, but then realized I couldn't because Kiki wasn't there. "Maybe later," I told him.

He dealt us each a hand of rummy. As we played, I kept looking across the yard where Daddy was showing Pie Face how to throw a knuckleball. Daddy kept rocking forward on the balls of his feet, the way he did when he got excited.

Sometimes I hated my daddy, but never had I felt like killing him until just at that moment. As soon as the thought came in, I felt ashamed.

I looked over to see that Granddaddy was watching me as I watched Daddy. I let the corners of my mouth loosen, trying to make my face less hateful so Granddaddy couldn't see what I was feeling. But from the way he studied me—his eyebrows drawn together, his hazel eyes narrowed—I could see that he knew exactly what I felt.

Finally, Daddy and Uncle Lester headed for the back door. Granddaddy got up, patted the back of my head, and followed them inside. Pie Face came over to me and took Granddaddy's empty seat.

"Wanna play gin?" he asked.

As we played, I could feel my confidence rise. Card-playing was a talent of mine. After beating Pie Face twice at gin, I was feeling pretty good. If only Daddy saw my skills at gin rummy to be as important as Pie Face's baseball skills, then maybe he wouldn't be so ashamed of me.

Pie Face said, "We should've brought some of that pound cake out here."

"I'll go get it," I said.

When I got to the back door, I was surprised to find it locked. I knocked a few times and was about to give up and go around front when Kiki opened the door.

She said, "I don't feel so good."

"Probably ate too much," I told her, stepping around her and into the house.

I went over to the fridge and found the cake. I set two big hunks of it on a napkin and was headed toward the back door when I heard Kiki coughing in the bathroom.

"Kiki?" I called.

When I nudged the bathroom door open, Kiki was down on her knees, puking her guts out. Sour-smelling vomit swam in the toilet water and lay on the linoleum.

I turned, intending to go and get Daddy, but a flash of red outside the bathroom window caught my eye. Stepping around Kiki, I moved to the window and looked out.

Daddy stood in the little drainage ditch in the side yard. Virginia Mitchum, the mama of one of Pie Face's friends who lived down the road, stood with Daddy, barefoot, her toes digging into the dirt. He had his arm around her. He whispered something in her ear, his lips brushing the side of her face.

Something stirred in my belly, and my cock moved slightly against my underwear. What was wrong with me? This seemed to happen only at the most embarrassing times—in the middle of Sunday school class or when a heavyset woman bent over in front of me at the grocery, stretching her dimpled legs.

I drew the curtains closed, wishing I was alone in the bathroom and that Virginia was naked. I had seen naked women in magazines, but never up close.

I turned from the window and stepped in something slippery.

Damn.

"Sorry, Pritchie." Kiki said.

I took a towel off a bathroom shelf, wetted it at the sink, and gave it to Kiki. She flushed the toilet and wiped her face with the towel.

Pie Face stepped into the doorway. "Where's the cake?" he asked. "Cain't be all gone."

What would Pie Face do if I told him Daddy was trying to get with Virginia, his friend's mama? Maybe he would kick Daddy's ass. The only reason I hadn't was because I wasn't big enough yet. *Please, God, let me grow big enough to dust him.*

"What's wrong with her?" Pie Face asked me. He looked down at the sink counter. "What's the cake doing in here, man? Gross."

Kiki had been using the towel to mop up the vomit. She stood up, tottered, as if her knees might buckle, and reached for a glass on the edge of the sink.

"Wait, hold up," Pie Face said. "That ain't yours, is it?" he asked her, gesturing at the glass. "Girl, that ain't no straight up orange juice. It's mostly vodka," he said, looking down at the nearly empty glass. He snatched it from her and poured the rest of it down the drain.

Pie Face walked back toward the kitchen and yelled, "Uncle Pritch! Kiki's throwing up!"

Kiki tried to hand me the soiled towel. I gestured to the basin, and she dropped it in there.

The screen door banged shut, and I heard snatches of the conversation between Pie Face, Lester, and Daddy. Daddy's voice was loudest, and I could imagine the angry look on his face.

"Why in the hell ain't you been watching your sister?" Daddy's voice came toward us, his feet banging down on the floor with each step.

I backed away from the bathroom door until my heels hit the side of the bathtub.

Daddy appeared in the doorway. "You gon' let her kill herself?!"

Kiki put her hands up over her ears and started to cry.

"I'm going to run her over to the hospital. She may have alcohol poisoning." Lester said.

"No need of a hospital. She's just throwing up is all, right?" Daddy said, glaring down at me. *"Right?"*

Anytime Daddy got scared, he got mad. He'd cussed up a storm the night Mama left. Cussed until his voice got hoarse.

Lester took Kiki's hand, and we all followed the two of them down the hall and outside onto the porch. Kiki bent over the porch railing and let loose another vomit.

Daddy went down the steps into the yard and paced back and forth in front of Kiki. "Get it all out, baby girl. Just let it all come up," he told her.

"Pritchard, we got to get her to a hospital. She may—"

"Would you shut your damn mouth up, Lester? That girl ain't got no alcohol poisoning."

There was silence in the yard as we all watched Kiki and Daddy. Then, Daddy broke the silence:

"Get in the car, Pritch. We're going home."

He scooped up Kiki and dropped her over his shoulder, like she was a bag of dog food. He went charging toward the car, taking those big strides of his, and I looked at Uncle Lester, hoping he'd step in and rescue us. But Lester just watched Daddy. Eliza came forward and blocked Daddy's path. As she begged for the keys, he nudged her aside.

Daddy put Kiki in the front seat and then rounded the hood to the driver's side. By the time I made it to the car, he'd roared the engine. I jumped in back, and he didn't even wait for me to get the door shut before he started backing down the driveway. The back tires got caught in a big rut and shook the car. Cursing loudly, Daddy hit the gas again, sending the back tires backward out of the rut and replacing them with the front ones. The front end of the car made a big KABLOOM when it rocked down into the ditch. Murray howled.

Finally, Daddy got us back onto the highway again. He kept squeezing the steering wheel, and I imagined him squeezing Virginia's tit. I thought I'd throw up, too.

I grabbed the handle and cranked my window down, trying to get rid of the sour mash smell.

The car swayed over the line every now and again. A few miles up the highway from our trailer, Daddy pulled the car off the road. He drove us down a gravel dirt road a ways and then cut the engine. He kept looking over at Kiki, who was wedged in the space between the door and seat. She hadn't moved since we got in the car, and I assumed she'd fallen asleep. Daddy leaned close to her, smoothed a plait back from her face, then felt of her forehead and cheek. I didn't realize I was holding my breath until he looked over his shoulder at me.

He laid his seat back so far that his head was in my lap.

"I know I never told you this, Pritch, but I'm sorry I'm such a disappointment as a father." He sighed, and I smelled his sour citrus breath. "But life ain't so bad with me, is it, son? Think back on it. Don't the good times outnumber the bad?"

Daddy closed his eyes, and pretty soon he was snoring softly. I slipped out of the car and up to the front passenger seat, where I pulled Kiki out. She wasn't much bigger than our dog Scooter, and I had no trouble carrying her, only I didn't know what exactly I was supposed to do. Maybe if I got us to the main highway I could flag someone down. Then what? I knew that Mama was staying with Aunt Rita, but I couldn't remember the phone number.

I carried Kiki down the road for a full minute before I realized she wasn't asleep. She looked up at me without blinking, like she was in a trance. I squatted and set her feet on the ground.

We were so close to the shoals I could smell the water—earthy and mossy. Bears flashed through my mind. They had been spotted in these woods before.

Something rolled over in the bushes beside us, and Kiki moved closer to me. She looked confused and tottered on her heels. I put my arm around her shoulders and she leaned against me as we walked. Even though it was warm out, she shivered.

The sun had gone down, and the sky had turned a purplish pink. Insects made a loud whirring sound. The moon was nice and bright that night, but the tops of the trees blocked most of the light. It would've been pretty if I hadn't been so afraid of the woods at dark.

"I didn't know we were so far from the highway, did you?" I asked.

She looked like she was fighting sleep. As we walked, she held me in a kind of side-hug, her hands clasping my hip bone. Every now and again, she squeezed me.

Remembering Daddy's talk about how Pearl came out at night was enough to make me shiver and tense my shoulders. I saw a flash of movement from the corner of my eye but didn't see a thing when I looked to our right.

"Didn't it seem we were pretty close to the highway when Daddy stopped the car?" I asked, talking only to hear my voice, to keep myself from thinking of bears with big teeth and claws. *Mauling.*

Then I saw her. Pearl. She stood off to our right in the woods, her hair loose and puffed out around her face in curls. She wore a long, white gown, cinched tight at her waist. Her figure was the kind that made Daddy grin when he saw it—wide hips and big tits.

Pearl's face was lit by the fire in front of her. The fire crackled and shot sparks into the air, like a fireworks display. She waved her hands in front of it, and the fire calmed itself, tapered down to only a few inches. Pearl lifted her arms up and drew herself onto tiptoes, bringing the flames as high as the treetops. Then she knelt before it, bringing her palms down to the ground, almost extinguishing the fire. I could barely see her face for a moment. When the fire was at its lowest, she looked over at me.

Run, run, run.

But my legs wouldn't move, except a light trembling as they shook.

She's your great-grandmama, Granddaddy Crawley's mama. She won't hurt you.

Time stopped. Or else I forgot it existed. I moved to the edge of the clearing. She stayed crouched, her palms resting on the ground. Large cheekbones gave her a masculine look, but her sloped, catlike eyes were as pretty as any I'd seen before or since. She was young, much younger than Daddy.

Pearl spoke to me, but her lips didn't move. Instead, she held my gaze, and I read the words right out of her head. *Every generation, one of us will kill one of our own. That can't be stopped. Every generation, a bloodshed.*

I must've looked scared then, because she said, *Don't be afraid. You're a good boy, Pritchard.*

It seemed she knew everything about me—my fear of being a runt forever, the embarrassing hard-ons, my hatred of my daddy.

I begged her, *Tell me what to do.*

And then, I was at the Granada again, looking down at Daddy, who still lay with his head against the headrest, sleeping soundly. My eyes went to a large rock that lay in the grass a few feet away. I could almost feel myself touching it, how cool it would feel in my hands after laying there under the trees for so long. The moss covering it might be littered with ants that would scatter and run up and down my fingers. I leaned toward the rock, grunted a little as I lifted it, then hefted it above my head.

I heard Pearl's voice again, this time ordering me: *Take care of your sister.*

I looked down at my side, but Kiki wasn't there.

Headlights came down the dirt road toward Kiki, who stood in the middle of the road.

Move, Kiki. Move! I wasn't sure if the words were in my head or if I yelled them. I was in one of those dreams where you need to run but can't.

The driver's tires made a crunching sound on the gravel as they came to a stop.

The woman driver got out and asked what we were doing out here in the woods. I recognized her as a woman who worked with my mama at the diner in town, but I couldn't remember her name. She stared at the rock in my hands, and I let it fall into a ditch along the side of the road.

The woman drove Kiki and me up the path to her house, where we sat silently together on her couch while she called our mother.

I stayed at the hospital all night with Mama and Kiki. Mama sat by Kiki's bed while she slept. I don't remember everything else, but I do remember Pearl. Sometimes I go a whole month without even remembering my daddy, but not a day goes by when I don't see Pearl commanding that fire or call up the image of her in that white gown.

I remember the fights afterward, how Daddy seemed to think it my fault that Kiki got ahold of the vodka. And I remember the cool day in November when Daddy put his clothes in the back of the old Ford and drove away from our double-wide for the last time. There was a finality to it. Though Mama had left half a dozen times, there was never a doubt that she'd come back to us. Daddy wasn't a come-back man, not for nothing.

Aunt Eliza was Daddy's last girlfriend. She was light-skinned, and my daddy always did love a light-colored woman. I can hear the things he probably said to her as he touched her, the way he complimented her skin.

Uncle Lester came home while Daddy was sitting out on the porch with Eliza one night. For years, I pictured myself on that porch. The headlights of Lester's pickup suddenly appear, spotlighting Daddy and Eliza. Daddy shields his eyes, jumps the railing as he struggles to button his jeans. Lester has a shotgun, kept one all the time on the back of his pickup. He shoots my daddy straight through the back as Daddy runs toward the highway, shirtless and with only one boot on.

Lester was the one called the law, said he'd seen a prowler running away from the porch. I can't attest to the truth of his statement, but it was enough to keep him out of the penitentiary.

Daddy was killed back when I was fourteen. I didn't cry when Mama told me about it. Instead, I remembered a moment I'd shared with Daddy and Pie Face. I must've been about eight years old. We were in Uncle Lester's backyard, and Pie Face had looked at me and said, "Race you to the tree." We took off running. The grass was wet, and we kept sliding over it. I pulled out ahead of him, wind slapping my mesh shorts against my knees. I looked over my shoulder just as he stumbled and fell onto the grass. I kept running. Daddy stood at the persimmon tree. When I tagged the tree, Daddy swept me up. I felt the world tilt as he swung me around, held me up by my ankles.

Gris-Gris

First, the tornado hit. Then, three days later, Lucy Boudreaux went missing. We all said she was a whirlwind (the Boudreaux girl, not the tornado).

Her real name was Lucinda, but she hated it. Wouldn't you? So everybody called her Lucy, which is an old lady's name, we think. We all went to school together. In those days, Lucy Boudreaux played ball on our team. Basketball. It's what our county was known for. *Girls'* basketball. We didn't just have a team. We had a stick. And we'd beat you with it. Best team in northeast Georgia, maybe even the whole country. Our gym still flies that state championship banner we won in '87.

God, that day she went missing was pure fall. The air—crisp enough to prickle you and make you hug yourself—smelled like burning leaves. The trees were every color from deep red to bright yellow. Back then, County Farm Road ran from Evan Myers clear to Three Forks. We drove up and down those roads in two pickup trucks, most of us sprawled on the trucks' beds, the wind cutting through our hair and chilling our skins. We were on another "cleanup pickup" to collect the debris—scratchy shingles and splintered wood—that had been strewn by the tornado. We liked the look of the insulation the most, how fluffy it was, how it felt like cotton candy on our fingertips.

Once we dumped the trash down at Bertrand's Sanitation, we went to the school to do our warm-ups. All twelve of us—minus Lucy—formed a line that wound around the three-point curve and snaked its way toward the half-court line.

"Where's Lucy?" asked Coach Newson, who could look at any line of us and immediately notice who wasn't there.

We smirked, hid our smiles behind our hands, grinned at the shiny floor.

"She must be with Coach Terrance," Kiara said to Coach Newson.

Under her breath, so that only we could hear, Kasha said, "Probably gettin' her back broke in."

We all knew Lucy and Terrance were hooking up. He was our new assistant coach that year and a junior at the local college. Lucy was a senior, our starting point guard, and one of our leading scorers. At an away game, some of us saw them together in the bed of his truck, her head on his shoulder, his hand over hers. At first none of us believed it. The year before, she'd dated one of us, Ashley Crawley, who had a pixie haircut and a great jump shot. You shoulda seen Ashley's face—eyes narrowed, nose flared out—when she saw Lucy and Terrance together on the bed of the truck.

By the time we'd finished our warm-ups, Lucy and Terrance still hadn't shown up. The bleachers began to fill with spectators. The other team—Jefferson High, which had only one really tall girl—walked past us. Coach Newson motioned for us to get into the locker room.

As Newson gave the pep talk, Lucy's mama knocked on the door and poked her head in. She wore her salt-and-pepper hair in long braids. "Where's Lucy?" she asked. Worry lines creased her forehead.

Coach Newson stepped out into the hallway to talk with Mrs. Boudreaux, but we all stayed quiet enough to hear. Lucy's mama said Lucy had left home that morning and come to the gym to shoot some hoops. She'd told her mama she'd see her at the game that night. Newson said he'd been in and out all day and hadn't seen her. We noticed he didn't tell Lucy's mama that Terrance wasn't around either.

During the game we kept looking toward the double doors on either side of the gym, hoping to see Lucy. But she never came. Terrance turned up alone. Something on him was always disheveled—his wild afro or his wrinkled clothes. That night, his jacket was buttoned up wrong so that one side hung lower than the other. He'd been a ball player himself in high school, and you'd know it by his tall, lanky frame—about six foot four—and those hands that could easily palm the ball. He came over to our bench and leaned into Coach Newson's ear. We could tell Newson was having none of it. His brows drew close together. He waved Terrance away and started yelling the play at Ashley, Lucy's backup point guard.

After the game (we won 76–61), we sat huddled together on the benches in the locker room and on the leather couch that sat in the center of the room. One of us had thought she'd seen Lucy walking on the side of the road the night before, but when called to, Lucy (or whoever it was) hadn't looked back. Someone else had called Lucy's house to ask about today's cleanup pickup, but Lucy's mama had said she was out.

"Y'all see Coach Terrance wander in late like dat?" asked Macy, a tall and thin dark-skinned girl who was best friends with Lucy.

We all stared at Macy, wide-eyed, our heads nodding up and down.

"What y'all think will happen to him?" Macy asked.

The boys' team must've scored, not just a basket but an amazing play—maybe an alley-oop or a three pointer—because the crowd erupted and chanted: "Raiders! Raiders!"

"Happen to him?" Ashley asked. "Why would anything happen to the golden child?"

Eddie Murphy was popular back then, and we'd all seen *The Golden Child* together in the theater. Ashley had been calling Terrance the golden child ever since, though there was no comparison between the child in the movie and Terrance. Ashley mocked Terrance's long-legged, loping walk, his way of sitting with his legs too wide apart, and all the attention he paid to Lucy.

"Maybe it was the curse," Ashley said, and the rest of us groaned.

Lucy and her family had moved to our town in north Georgia from Louisiana, and Lucy was the most superstitious person any of us had ever seen. She always carried a little pouch, and during games she tied the pouch to her bra strap. She called it a gris-gris and said hers was for good luck but that some used gris-gris to cast spells on enemies.

"Then how you know yours is for luck and not a curse?" we asked her.

"'Cause my granny made it for me," she said with an eyeroll.

And it must've been good luck, some of us decided, because we hadn't lost a game since she'd joined our team and had even hung that state championship banner in '87.

"You never heard of voodoo?" Lucy had demanded, trying to coax us all into carrying a gris-gris. "Y'all Black, ain't y'all?"

"We don't know nothin' bout no jungle voodoo. Girl, is you crazy?" Ashley had asked her, and we all cracked up.

We gathered our things and went out to the stands to watch the boys' game. Near the end of the fourth quarter, when we were satisfied that the boys' twenty-point lead was enough to secure the W, we went outside, piled into the two pickups and drove down to the Hardee's for burgers and fries. We nodded to our classmates, both those who worked there and those who came to hang out.

And then Terrance walked in.

We all watched him as he stood in the doorway, his eyes searching every corner of the restaurant and then landing at the two tables we'd pushed together near the middle. His eyes moved from one of us to the next. Kasha waved him over, but he turned and went out the door, followed closely by Macy. If you'd seen the look on Macy's face, you'd know why we all followed her and Terrance out of the restaurant.

In the parking lot, we chased Macy's red coat as she tracked Terrance all the way to his car, which was parked near the dumpster. We saw the flailing of her arms, the blur of them as she came at him, how he put up his own arms to block her blows. "Where is she?" Macy kept asking. "Where?!"

We watched, most of us stunned, as Terrance locked her arms behind her back. She struggled against him another few seconds, and then collapsed into sobs. He whispered to her, something like, "I don't know. I don't know. It wasn't me . . ."

After that, the speculation and conspiracy theories ramped up. Some folks said she was walking along the side of the highway the morning she disappeared and was probably picked up, though we didn't believe that for one second. No way would Lucy hitchhike. Some suspected Coach Newson had something to do with her disappearance, but we knew Coach. He'd never hurt any of us. The most popular theory was that Terrance had killed her and dumped her somewhere, until it was confirmed that he was taking the GRE in Atlanta that morning, that she was safely at home at breakfast with her family while he would've been en route to the test, and that he was at the testing center for several hours. Coach had known in advance that Terrance would be late to our game.

For months, we searched for her. Hung "Have you seen me?" posters on telephone poles and grocery store bulletin boards.

People left hateful messages for Coach Newson, accused him of pedophilia and violence after someone dug up an old charge from when Newson had been accused of assaulting a much younger ex-girlfriend. He quit the team over it, though he never admitted the reason for his resignation. We'd see him around town, working in the insurance firm his brother worked in, or standing in line at the grocery.

Our team lost. Then lost again. And again. Didn't make playoffs that year. Before every game, we'd pray to stay healthy, pray to play well, and pray for Lucy. In hindsight, we wanted her home for purely selfish reasons. We wanted her enthusiasm, how she knew the exact right thing to say to each of us before a game. We wanted her for us, our joy, the excitement we felt when she sank a three after popping the ball into the air, quick as lightning off the dribble. We wanted to say that she was a Division I prospect from our school and for her to help us hang another state championship banner during her senior year.

One day, near the end of that terrible ball season, the news broke. Her skull and a leg bone had surfaced, floating peacefully, out at Harmony Shoals. The medical examiner called it an accidental drowning.

The town gathered in our gym for her funeral. Mrs. Boudreaux had told everyone to wear white, and Lucy's grandmother had given each of us a little gris-gris sachet that we pinned to our warm-up jackets. Coach Newson had quit the team by then, but he came down to the line we formed under the basketball hoop. That must've been the last time we were all together with Coach and Terrance. We retired her jersey right then, and it soared up toward the rafters. They put it next to our championship banner from the year before.

Some said it was so sad that we had no body to bury, though others of us said it was better to not see our friend in a coffin and have that memory overtake the living memories. Her folks decided to say a prayer over the spot in Harmony Shoals where they'd found her bones. After the jersey ceremony, the long procession to the Shoals took almost longer than we could bear. Sitting in the backs of the two pickups, we must've looked like the saddest girls in the world. When we finally came to the place where someone had stuck a marker in the ground to remember her, Coach and Terrance helped us bring out our gift to Lucy: a humongous wreath we'd made using white ribbon and artificial daffodils. We carefully lay the wreath on the earth. Some of us worried it would blow away, that no one would get to enjoy it for very long. That's when Terrance looped a bungee cord through the wreath and tied it to a nearby tree.

Mrs. Boudreaux said the prayer, and she just sounded tired, not sad anymore, maybe relieved that she could stop searching, stop lying awake worrying about Lucy.

Some of us moved away. Several of us got college scholarships, became teachers and coaches and business owners and even a lawyer. We scattered, but most stayed around the Peach State. Every year, there was a pancake breakfast fundraiser for the team, and it eventually got named for Lucy Boudreaux. That made us sad. Lucy deserved more than her name attached to the pancake breakfast. She deserved something bigger, a gym named after her or a scholarship fund.

The weekend before she went missing, we'd all gone down to Harmony Shoals together. It was one of those old-fashioned parks that had a covered bridge leading into it. Once in the water, we stood on the smooth, hot rocks and looked down to see the murky outlines of our feet. Lucy talked about what she would do on graduation day, what she'd wear, how she'd bop across the stage. She, like most of us, wanted to go to college, to marry, raise babies. Under that sun, we all knew, Lucy included, that we would get what we wanted. Everything had come together, and we all rode on a current of youth and newness and the future lay before us, stretched out, endlessly.

Kasha and Ansley

As he drove us home from my granny's funeral, Jack reached up to adjust the bill of his ball cap. His chin-length black hair peeked out around the edges of the cap. Sun had darkened his light brown skin. Jack is Native American, and he is only a shade lighter than me.

The closer we got to home, the more the chicken houses thinned out. Gradually, the land turned to dense forest. When Jack rounded the cluster of cedar trees at the start of my driveway, an old-fashioned VW Beetle came into view. Most of the green paint was scratched off of it, replaced by a layer of rust.

Jack stopped the Silverado in the middle of my long driveway. "Expecting company, Ansley?" he asked me.

"I don't even recognize that car."

My sister, Kasha, came out of my house and walked toward the VW. She opened the hatch, removed a suitcase. When she saw the truck she hung back, waiting for us to come into the yard. I hadn't seen Kasha in about six years, and there she was, waving at me.

Jack pulled down into the gravel driveway beside the Beetle. We got out of the truck. Kasha came forward and held her arms out, but when I did not step into her embrace she squeezed my shoulder instead.

Kasha's faded yellow T-shirt advertised a farmers' market, and across the chest were a papaya, a mango, and a bunch of bananas. She wore jeans and a flowered headband. Her black hair was streaked with red highlights. The ever-present grin and the bright primary colors made her look younger than her twenty-nine years.

"You okay?" she asked.

I realized I had one palm to my chest, like people do in movies when they're having a heart attack.

"What are you doing here?" I asked her.

She laughed. "Good to see you, too, little sis." She turned to Jack and introduced herself.

"Where've you been?" I asked her.

"Cincinnati. The lawyer got ahold of me yesterday and told me about Granny." She paused and studied me, as if she wanted to see how I was doing with Granny's death. I waited for the customary "How are you holding up?" But Kasha didn't offer it.

"I'm meeting with the lawyer tomorrow, and I came by here because I need a place to stay . . . ," she trailed off as she tried to read my face.

"You mean for tonight?" I asked her.

There were two cardboard moving boxes on the back seat of her car. When she caught me looking at them, she said, "A few weeks, maybe a month?"

Kasha had been bad about not returning Granny's phone calls. She hadn't visited in years, not even when Granny offered to wire her money for the trip.

Kasha said, "I could stay in the cottage."

"Cottage is rented. He's the boarder," I said, gesturing at Jack.

"What about Granny's room?" she asked.

"Her stuff's still in there, haven't cleaned it out yet. And the guest room's used for storage."

"The couch?" Her eyes went to Jack and then back to me. "The screened porch?" She opened her mouth again, but shut it without speaking.

They both stared at me.

Granny had raised me to look out for family, to basically have compassion for anyone, no matter how badly they'd treated me. I was my grandmama's daughter.

"I guess I could make up Granny's room for you."

Jack started to help her unload the Beetle. I walked into the house and went straight for the bag of chocolate-covered peanuts in the drawer beside the stove. Holding a few of them between my tongue and the roof of my mouth, I closed my eyes and sighed.

Kasha and Jack brought in her suitcase, the boxes, and a small carry-on bag. I settled on the couch and stared at the blank TV screen. When we were kids, we watched *Adventures in Babysitting* on this TV so often we had it memorized. We'd dance and sing along with the Crystals' song "And Then He Kissed Me." Kasha blew bubbles at me from a little plastic wand. I jumped up and down. Soap burned my eyes when the bubbles burst against my eyelids and cheeks.

Kasha rolled her suitcase over to where I sat on the couch. She stood by the armrest and stared down at me a second. I'm an emotional person, and I struggle to keep my expressions neutral. Kasha has always had this ability to study me a few seconds and read my mind. It's *annoying.* I turned my face away from her, and she rolled her suitcase over to the loveseat, sat down, and removed a package of peanuts from the suitcase. "How long have you lived in the cottage?" she asked.

"Almost a year now," Jack said. He put the second cardboard box atop the first one and sat by me on the couch.

Kasha started to shell the peanuts. She piled the cracked hulls on my coffee table.

She looked over at Jack, studied him carefully for a moment, and then said, "I was good friends with a Mexican woman at my last job."

This wasn't the first time Jack had been mistaken for Hispanic. Once, when the cable guy had come to Jack's cottage to install a new receiver box, he'd said something to Jack in Spanish.

"I'm Lumbee," Jack corrected him.

"He wasn't trying to offend you, you know," I said to Jack after the cable guy left. "He just saw that you have dark skin and black hair."

"You have dark skin and black hair, Ansley. Do you speak Spanish?" he asked in his best smart-aleck voice.

"I'm Black. I don't look like I speak Spanish."

"Sure you do. I've met some Cubans who could be your close cousins."

There was no winning an argument with that man.

I waited for Jack to explain to Kasha that he wasn't Mexican, but he didn't.

"So what do y'all do for fun around here, Annie?" asked Kasha.

My nickname threw me off a beat. Nicknames, in my opinion, are reserved for those closest to us, not estranged family members.

"I've just been working. I'm not the best person to ask about places to go out."

"What about your boyfriend? Where do you hang out?" she asked Jack.

What made Kasha think we were a couple? Jack and I were close, and I felt a relationship developing, but it hadn't happened yet. Even so, I had leaned on him a lot this past week. He'd helped prep for the funeral and sat next to me at Granny's wake, things *Kasha* should've helped me through.

If Kasha's assumption bothered him at all, Jack didn't show it. He said, "There's a bar called Finnegan's in town. I hang out there sometimes."

Kasha kept cracking the shells open, picking out the meat and dropping the hulls onto the table. Bits of the hulls and the skins fell on the carpet. She didn't seem to notice.

At dusk Jack stood, said good night, and went out the front door.

I went into Granny's room. Her bed was still neatly made, the patchwork quilt tucked back. I lay down and buried my face in her pillow, smelled the oil she'd always used in her hair. Coconut.

"Do you need—"

I jumped. When I turned around Kasha was standing in the doorway, frowning at me.

"—my help with anything?" she asked.

"No. I'll get you some fresh sheets."

From the hall closet, I gathered sheets, a comforter, and a spare pillow. When I got back to the bedroom, she was standing at Granny's dresser, admiring the scarves tied over the dresser mirror. She ran her fingers along a bright red one and then untangled it from the others. Watching herself in the mirror, she wound the scarf around her neck and knotted it at her throat. Kasha raised her eyes to my reflection in the mirror. She said, "Remember D. W. Kennedy?" When I nodded, she continued, "He eventually moved up to Cincinnati to stay with me. We married, but I had it annulled after a few months."

D.W. was her high school boyfriend. He belittled her any time they disagreed or any time he was in a bad mood for whatever stupid reason. Granny had even thrown D.W. out of our house one time for talking down to Kasha.

She came over and stood on the other side of the bed. I stretched the fitted sheet around the last corner of the mattress.

"We were staying together in Cincinnati. I left this morning, just packed my stuff and drove away," Kasha said.

"Thought you said it was annulled after a few months?"

"Yeah, but we've been on-again and off-again for years."

I carried Granny's sheets down to my room and dropped them in the hamper.

"Granny used to keep a set of bunk beds in here for us," Kasha said.

I turned to find her standing in my bedroom doorway, still wearing the red scarf. The red highlights in her hair somehow looked tasteful against the scarf and that silly, flowered headband.

Kasha walked over to the corner where the bunk beds used to be. Her fingers grazed the wall, no doubt looking for the spot where she'd carved "Kasha and Ansley" into the drywall. She said, "I've missed you, Annie. But after so much time passed, I didn't know if you'd want to hear from me again." She began to cry. "And now Granny's gone and I never got to say goodbye."

She regretted not spending more time with Granny and me; I was sure of that. But I also knew her well enough to see her tears were there to garner pity.

"This house is mine. Mine *alone,*" I told her.

"I know that. I'm not trying to take it from you," she said. "You were always the best of us two—smart, reliable, focused. You deserve this place and anything else Granny left you."

I said, "She didn't leave you much, just a few thousand dollars."

"The lawyer told me over the phone," she said, rubbing the tears away with the back of her hand.

"I'm not gonna kick you out, Kasha."

She hugged me for a second, released me when I tensed my shoulders. A pitiful look came into her eyes then. She turned her attention to my dresser and ran a finger over the plaque I got a couple of years ago at the bank. It was awarded to me for my work as a loan processor.

"Why did you leave us?" I asked. My voice caught in the middle of the sentence, and I couldn't look her in the eye. "You could've come back. You could've kept in touch."

Kasha ran her fingers over the edge of the dresser. She'd played piano when we were kids, and she used to practice her scales that way, running her fingers over countertops and tables. But just then she didn't look at the dresser as though it were a piano. She was looking at me. She said, "I don't fit here, not in this family. I'm not conservative and I'm not Christian." She pointed at the painting of a cross that hung above my headboard. "Plus, I didn't want to hang around Muscadine with you and Granny and get old before my time."

"So that's how you see me. Old at twenty-six?"

She didn't respond for a minute, but then she said, "You're younger than me, but you've always been the mature one. And I do see you as very judgmental, like Granny. You wouldn't've wanted me to hang around you, not with the stuff I was into."

"What stuff?"

Kasha loosened the scarf and used one end of it to fan her face. "The telephone works both ways, Annie." She laughed bitterly. "Don't pretend you wanted some fornicating atheist of a sister in your life. Even Granny stopped calling when she realized I didn't want to come back here. You both gave up on me."

Kasha lifted the lid of my jewelry box. "Für Elise" began to play. I slipped off the gold watch Granny had given me for my high school graduation and put it in one corner of the jewelry box.

Kasha said, "I do want to be close to you again, Annie. I know it's hard to forgive, I'm just asking you to try is all."

I said, "If one thing keeps me out of heaven, it'll be my grudge-holding."

I didn't realize how much those words would sting until I looked into Kasha's eyes.

Feeling the need to relieve some of that pain, I said, "I missed you, Kasha. I *did* miss you."

She pumped both fists in the air, a gesture I recognized. When we were kids, the air fists meant she'd talked me into some chore neither of us wanted to do—cleaning the fridge or scrubbing the rim of the toilet bowl.

I said, "I'm going out to Jack's."

I walked through the living room, right past the peanut shells, resisted the urge to vacuum. Let Kasha clean it up. It was her mess.

Jack's cottage sat behind my house. The cottage was originally a toolshed that Granny expanded and decided to rent out as a way to make some extra money after retirement. The cottage had a fresh coat of yellow paint and a tiny front porch barely big enough for Jack's two chaise lounge chairs. Jack sat in one of them. Two cans of Co-Cola rested on the porch floor beside him. Once I'd lowered myself into the other chaise, he handed me one. I pulled the tab and took a sip.

"How'd you know to have a cold one waiting for me? Am I that predictable?"

Jack said, "So what's got you more pissed? Her showing up, or her not contacting you for so long?"

"I'm more angry at her for not being in my life, but I also know she can be difficult. She's messy, flighty, and doesn't pull her weight. What if she doesn't get a job and ends up here for the next year?"

"I get it. I've been on my own for years now, so having a roommate would bug me."

"Maybe this is just me being selfish. I can't even welcome my own sister home. If Granny were here she'd be so happy to see Kasha."

Jack's eyes closed slowly. He didn't respond for a few seconds, but then he said, "Your grandma could do no wrong. You were lucky to have her."

"So was Kasha, but she never knew it. Mama and Daddy died Kasha's senior year in high school. She finished the school year here with Granny and me, and then took off for college in Cincinnati that fall."

When Jack didn't reply, I looked over at him. He'd drifted off to sleep.

I put my head back against the chaise. Kasha and I had begun to grow apart right after our parents passed away in a car crash. Kasha became disrespectful. Granny struggled to control her.

Jack said, "I've seen you, sitting out on your porch after dark, looking up at the sky. I'd like to come over, stargaze with you sometime." His eyes were still closed.

Our armrests touched. He smelled like pine trees. His cottage was surrounded by them, and he was always working in the yard or fishing the stream down in the woods.

Why was I holding my breath? I let it out softly.

"You wanna come inside a minute?" he asked.

We drained the last of our Cokes. He pushed the door open and let me enter first. The house was clean but a little messy. A coffee mug and a few newspapers lying around gave it a lived-in look.

My favorite part of the cottage was the old-fashioned chandelier that Granny had hung just over the center of the living room. The ceilings were very low, and the chandelier hung low enough that taller people had to duck under it, but I was short, and Jack was only a few inches taller.

Jack took off his ball cap and tossed it onto the couch. Half his face was in shadow, but the other part glowed under the chandeliered light. I had always thought him handsome, and the light made him more so.

I went over to the bookcase on the wall opposite the door. Jack had more books than anyone I knew—a full floor-to-ceiling bookcase in the living room, and two other big bookshelves in his bedroom. He was into Native American history. Most of the books on his shelves were biographies of Indian leaders and US presidents.

"You should read the Tapahonso poems," Jack said. His eyes widened and he came over to stand in front of me. He looked like he wanted to jump up and down.

"I like this side of you," I said.

"What side?"

"Sweet, excited."

I took a novel from the shelf and flipped toward the end. "I always read the ending of a book first," I said.

He stared at me. "Why?" he asked.

"I hate surprises," I told him. I put the book back on the shelf. "Jack, you said once that you wanted to be a history teacher. Still plan to?"

He nodded. "I do think about it. But I've been an electrician for almost ten years now. It'd be strange to give that up and go back to school. And I always did get bored in classrooms."

He glanced down at my lips, and for a moment I was certain he'd kiss me. When he didn't, I covered his mouth with mine. Our bodies pressed together, and when we walked half-blind through the living room, his hand banged against the chandelier as he pulled his shirt over his head. The chandelier swayed, shifted the light, made the whole room tilt.

We heard a noise out on the front porch. Jack started toward the door, then took my hand and tried to walk me into the bedroom.

"Don't you want to see who's outside?" I asked, holding back.

He pulled his shirt back on and went to the door. Shelby Stover stood on the little porch, her hand raised to knock again. She wore short shorts and a tank top, and her red hair was pulled back in a high ponytail.

"Hey, honey," she said, smiling up at Jack. When her eyes landed on me, she dropped the playful tone. "Hey, Ansley," she said, looking back at Jack with a question in her eyes.

I stepped around her and headed home.

After my shift at the bank on Monday, I went by the grocery to do the week's shopping. When I got home that evening, Jack and Kasha were standing in my backyard. A Black man in a blue baseball cap stood with them. D. W. Kennedy, Kasha's asshole ex-husband.

The three of them saw me bend to unload the groceries, and they walked up the hill toward me.

"Guess what?" Kasha asked, planting a kiss on my cheek.

I've never been the huggy, kissy sort. But Kasha is different—very affectionate. I imagined that before long she'd be pecking Jack's cheek, too, if she hadn't already.

"Jack and I are going to start a garden," she said.

I looked at Jack. Months ago I'd mentioned a garden to him.

"We'll have squash, beans, watermelon, maybe even corn," she said. "We better hurry and get the seeds in the ground. It's June already."

The plastic handles dug into my arms. I set the grocery bags down on the hood of my Toyota and twisted my wrists back and forth to relieve tension.

Kasha noticed me watching D.W. and said, "You two remember each other, right?"

The smile on D.W.'s lips didn't meet the expression in his brown eyes. He studied me, probably trying to see what I remembered about him. He was tall and powerfully built. He wore baggy jeans and black boots. I stared at him longer than would be polite.

I picked up the bags and went into the house, where I was met by the smell of onions and some sort of pepper, maybe cayenne. On the stove, a pot of stew simmered. I set the bags on the kitchen table. Jack and Kasha came in, toting the rest of the groceries. Jack began to fill the fridge while Kasha went to the sink to wash her hands. She picked up a wooden spoon and tenderly stirred the pot.

Kasha looked over her shoulder at me, said, "D.W.'s staying for dinner. And you're staying too, right, Jack?" she asked him.

"Smells so good," he said. "I can't say no."

Aside from D.W., Jack was the last person I wanted to see. Last night and this morning I kept replaying Shelby's arrival at Jack's cottage. Jack and Shelby used to go around together. She was a nice girl, and I liked her. She'd been friendly with me all through high school. Last year when our first boarder moved out and Granny put the ad in the paper about a cottage for rent, Shelby was the one to call and say that her boyfriend, Jack, wanted to rent it. She'd introduced us to him. But a couple of months ago she stopped coming around. I thought they'd broken up.

Jack took a carton of eggs and a package of cheddar cheese to the fridge.

I said, "I've got it from here, y'all. Go on back to your garden planning."

"I can help you put the groceries up, Ansley. It's no problem," Jack offered. He closed the fridge and went back to the bags on the table.

"No. Just *stop.*"

Kasha looked at Jack, tilted her head to the side and raised her eyebrows. Jack shrugged at her.

He went out into the yard and stood talking to D.W. under the pecan tree. D.W. lit a cigarette and offered the pack to Jack, but Jack shook his head.

I said, "I thought you were done with D.W.? What's he doing here?"

Kasha raised the wooden spoon and let it hover over the pot. "He drove down from Cincinnati. We're not together," she said. "But he wants to reconcile."

"You want *him* in your life? That's something you really need to reconsider."

She rolled her eyes and turned back to the pot. "Thanks, Mama," she said.

The urge to grab her hair and pull her to the floor came over me so strongly that I almost reached my hand out. She used to call me mama whenever she thought I was being too bossy or cross. Fact is, I was born old. Responsible and mature as early as elementary school, I did my homework at the kitchen table right after school without Mama and Daddy even having to ask. My dolls and stuffed animals were neatly placed in the toy box at the end of each play session. But Kasha was different. As a teenager, she loved talking on the phone for hours with her basketball teammates and all her other friends, and she had lots of them, something I never managed.

"You know," she said, "D.W.'s not that different from Jack. Both work with their hands. Both—"

"They're nothing alike," I said, watching the two men from the window.

"You think Jack's perfect?" Kasha asked. "Get a brain, baby girl."

Kasha opened the kitchen door and called the men in to dinner.

I went to the bathroom and washed up.

When I came back to the table, everyone was seated already. The stew was beef chunks, carrots, and potatoes seasoned with onions and pepper. I was impressed with it, especially because I had never known Kasha to be a good cook. I realized how little I knew about my sister. What had she studied in college? Did she graduate?

"You want to run with us to town for seeds tomorrow, Annie?" Jack asked.

I pointed at Jack and Kasha. "I guess y'all are taking the garden project away from me."

"We're not taking it from you. We just want to help, that's all," Jack said.

"I can manage it on my own."

In the silence that followed my words, D.W. belched softly and Jack cleared his throat. I finished the last of my stew and took my bowl to the sink. When I came back to the table, my watch was gone. I lifted the placemat where I'd set it, but only the cream-colored tablecloth looked up at me. No watch.

"What is it?" Jack asked.

"My watch is gone," I said, looking at D.W. "Did you see it?" I asked him.

He shook his head.

"You went to wash your hands. Could you have left it on the sink?" Kasha asked.

I went to the bathroom to look, and Kasha followed me in there. As soon as we were alone, she said, "Why'd you look at D.W.? That was incredibly rude."

"The watch was sitting right there beside him. Now it's gone."

"That *doesn't mean* he stole it."

"We got it, Annie," Jack called to me from the hallway.

When I came out of the bathroom, he was standing in the kitchen doorway, dangling my watch from his pointer finger. I slipped it off his finger and onto my wrist.

"It was sitting on the floor beside your chair," Jack said.

As I fastened the clasp, I bumped the screen door open with my hip and went out to the screened porch. The summer night was muggy. I sat on the wicker loveseat and listened to the voices coming from the kitchen. Jack and Kasha laughed as dishes rattled and silverware tinged. D.W. stood in the kitchen window, dishrag over his shoulder, and watched me.

Before long, the three of them came out to the screen porch.

"We're gonna go have another look at the garden spot, unless you're banning us?" Jack teased. "C'mon," he said, taking me by the arm.

I followed the three of them down the porch steps. When we came to the little patch of land I'd told Jack I wanted to set aside for a garden, D.W. turned to face Kasha. He rubbed his hands over her cheeks and hair. He leaned down and kissed her forehead. I'd never seen him this way with her. The boy I remembered was sullen and quick-tempered.

Jack said to me, "I'm going to turn the field after work on Wednesday." He chewed his bottom lip, like he did when he was reading. His hands moved around, telling me which crops should go where, pausing to see if I agreed.

As we walked back to the porch, Jack said, "Are you mad at me about Shelby?" A second earlier he had been talking about squash, but now his eyebrows were drawn together as he studied me.

We sat down on the porch steps.

"Nothing happened last night with her. She left right after you did," he said, and then, "I don't want to keep pretending there's nothing between you and me, Ansley. And I'm bringing it up now because now is when you're so pissed you can't even have dinner without storming off. That's so *you.* You hold everything in until you can't take it anymore and then you blow up." He smirked and bumped his shoulder against mine. "You know, your grandma wanted me for you. She loved me."

I snorted. "What a way to hook up with me. Use my dead grandma as leverage."

This was a milestone for me. It was the first time I'd thought about Granny without feeling sadness.

"I didn't mean it like that," he said.

"I know."

He looked off into the distance as he spoke again. "Your grandma interviewed me once. She asked all these questions about my future."

"What'd you say?"

"Said I'm a hard worker with a nest egg."

I reached out and ran a finger over the tiny hole at the neck of his T-shirt.

"Said I'm looking to buy some land in Hart County," Jack said.

My finger froze on the back of his neck.

"Unless you want me to stay around here," Jack said. His eyes demanded an answer to a question he hadn't properly asked.

"Yes," I told him. "I want you here."

Over in the side yard, Kasha leaned in through the open window of D.W.'s truck and kissed him goodnight.

I hadn't worked a garden since my daddy turned the field when I was in elementary school. Back then I wasn't old enough to understand garden work. I simply followed Granny and Daddy outside and watched them. On so many of those dusky summer evenings, I fell asleep on the screened porch to the sound of Daddy's hoe pulled slowly back and forth over the earth.

This time around, I had Jack and Kasha to guide me. Kasha had helped plant a community garden in Cincinnati, and Jack had gardened as a boy with his mama up in North Carolina.

After the first long Saturday of hoeing and planting, I felt it in my back and legs. I never knew gardening could be such strenuous work.

"It gets better once you get in shape," Kasha promised me. "Before long you'll dream of fresh vegetables and dirt under your nails."

And she was right. After a few weeks had gone by, I often spent my whole shift at work longing to be in the garden.

We usually worked in the evenings when the sun was low. Light and wind played over the distant trees. Everything smelled fresh and clean. I even grew used to the peppery smell of the natural pesticide Kasha made.

We had a bunny rabbit that nibbled our cabbage plants. I saw him hopping away into the woods some afternoons when I drove in from work.

"I've seen the little devil," Jack said one evening. "If I ever spot his butt from the window, I'll get him with my rifle."

"You wouldn't!" Kasha said.

"What should I do then? Let him eat up all our crops?" Jack said. "I'd love to have his ass in a stew."

It became a joke with us. Kasha would complain that the bunny had nibbled the cabbage leaves, and Jack would make morbid jokes about killing it. After a few days of this, Jack drove home with his truck bed loaded down with a critter fence.

Working with Kasha and Jack made me realize how lonely I'd been before they came into my life. My friend Jenny had moved away and married almost a year before. Once Jenny left, I had only Granny. Though Granny was good company, you couldn't tell her a dirty joke or even swear around her. Fuddy-duddy, that's what Kasha always called her.

For our garden, Jack and Kasha chose tomato, cabbage, squash, cucumber, and okra plants. Jack liked watermelon, and though it had never been my favorite, I wanted to plant it just because it reminded me so much of Granny. When I was little, I'd picked a watermelon off a vine and tried to carry it up to the house to show it off to Mama and Daddy. I made it halfway up the back porch steps and dropped it. I rolled the busted melon down the steps and into the grass in an attempt to hide it. Granny teased me about it for years. "Remember when you busted that melon, girl?" she'd say.

On the August day that I walked out to find tiny watermelons on Jack's vines, I cried.

"What's wrong?" Kasha asked.

"Just reminds me of Granny."

She looked like she wanted to hug me, but she didn't dare. She no doubt remembered her attempts at closeness from when she'd first moved in. How I'd rejected her. I regretted it just then. I wanted a good cry, a hug, and to reminisce about the family we'd lost. But I was raised by Mama and Daddy and Granny, three folks who scoffed at sentiment, so I never learned that showing strong emotion is acceptable. I'd always thought of Daddy, Mama, and Granny as saintly. How strange it was to admit they had flaws! And that I did, too.

One day, not long after we'd fenced our vegetables, the three of us cut okra together. In a hushed voice from across the row, Kasha said, "Look."

I turned and saw a deer standing a few steps behind me. He had a large rack of antlers. I'd heard stories of deer being so people-friendly nowadays that they would walk right up to you. I froze. He blinked, licked his lips. I picked up a hoe and shook it toward him. He bounded off into the woods.

"Are you all right?" Kasha asked.

When I turned, I saw that she'd asked the question of Jack, who stood at the end of the row. Red-faced and sweaty, he drew his arm up to wipe his face. He nodded at Kasha without saying a word.

"Jack," I said, going over to him. "You okay?"

"I'm all right," Jack said, shooing me away. His hands shook, and his chest heaved up and down. Jack picked up a basket of tomatoes and okra and started toward the porch with them. His shoulders slumped forward, and he no longer walked in relaxed, confident strides.

Once when I had ridden with him into town, a car almost side-swiped us. Jack turned red-faced and sweaty then, too. He mentioned anxiety attacks that day in the car, but when I tried to probe for more information, he dropped the subject. He undoubtedly thought his anxiety showed weakness. To say that Jack was a macho man would be an understatement.

As Jack and I lay in bed together that night, I said, "Jack, you scared me this afternoon."

We lay on our sides facing each other. When he didn't answer, I said, "I'm talking about the deer, and the—"

"I know what you're talking about."

"Well?"

"Well, what?" he asked, looking me in the eyes. "You think I should see a head doctor?"

"I'm not calling you crazy, I just think your panic attacks could be controlled better if you got some sort of help."

Jack chuckled, but in a sad way. "Look, I've been living with this my whole life. All that happens is I get a little nervous sometimes. Hell, it only happens once a year or two. I don't think taking pills and talking to some quack doctor can change it. Nervousness's not really a big deal anyway."

"It's more than nervousness. You should've seen yourself today. You—"

He pushed himself up to a sitting position so fast he startled me. "Just shut up about it, Annie." He flung his legs over the side of the bed and sat there, his back turned to me. "Goddamn it," he muttered.

Damn *you.*

I got up, went through the kitchen and out to the screen porch. The moon was so bright that I could faintly see bright squashes and tomatoes down in the garden. When I turned to sit on the porch's loveseat, I was startled to see Kasha there. Cellophane crackled. She raised her hand to her mouth. As I sat down beside her, I saw that she was eating my chocolates.

I put my hand out, and she poured a few into it.

An apple, a bag of chips, a container of onion dip, and a bottle of Mountain Dew sat on the table in front of us.

"Doggone," I said. "Anything left in the fridge?" When she didn't even crack a smile, I said, "Thought I heard D.W. come in?"

"He's staying here tonight," she said. "You don't mind, do you?"

I shrugged. "You live here, too."

I took a potato chip from the bag and munched it.

"Is Jack staying the night?"

"Yes, unless he's still pissed at me."

I felt her eyes on me, but she didn't speak. Maybe she'd had a disagreement with D.W. Why else would she be sitting out here while he was there in her bedroom?

I used to measure how close I was to a person by how long we could sit together in comfortable silence. This was the first time I'd shared a comfortable silence with Kasha, whereas Granny and I could sit out on this porch together for hours without speaking.

"You look like Granny," I said, not really knowing the words would come out until they did. "In this light you do."

She shook her head. "Nope, I look like you."

I heard the soft sound of her lips parting across her teeth when she smiled.

Kasha was full of surprises. I'd thought she'd be a bad roommate, but she'd proved me wrong. Though she left dental floss over the shower curtain rod and little gobs of toothpaste in the wash basin, sharing a house with her wasn't bad. She'd found a job as a receptionist at a car dealership in town. She even offered to pay rent. Most importantly, it was nice to have someone to share things with. If I had a hard time at work, I could come home and play cards with Kasha or bake bread for us to share. Those things ward off loneliness.

I took a few more gulps of the fresh air, said goodnight to Kasha, and went back to the bedroom. Jack stared at me as I walked toward the bed.

I stretched out on my back beside him. He rolled onto his side, propped up on one elbow, his face hovering above mine. He said, "I love you."

My heart stopped. "How'd you go from being angry at me to loving me?"

He rolled his eyes. "I was never mad at you. I had planned to tell you how I felt tonight. Was set to do it before you started talking therapy and medication."

When I didn't respond, he said, "You're so much like my mama. She always showed me how she felt, but she rarely said it. I know you love me, Annie. Not saying it doesn't keep you from feeling it."

The kitchen door closed softly. The fridge opened, and then a cabinet. I imagined Kasha putting her snacks away and making her way to her bedroom.

"What am I going to do when you get tired of me?" I asked Jack.

"What?"

"I mean, what if I say 'I love you' and then we break up? Or what if you die tomorrow?"

He said, "So you refuse to tell me you love me just because we might break up someday?"

"I know how stupid it sounds, but it's a real fear for me," I said. "Besides, you're obligated to tell me you love me," I teased him. "I own your house."

His eyebrows shot up and then down, which meant he was ready with a smart-aleck reply. Before he could respond, we heard low moans from Granny's room.

I looked at Jack. We watched each other's faces, our ears cocked toward the wall. A guttural Oh-hhhhh-hhhhh came from the bedroom, which sent Jack into quiet hysterics. He clutched his chest. He said, "Old D.W.'s having a good time, ain't he?"

I'd seen the lust on Kasha's face every time she was near D.W. The man couldn't carry on much conversation without pausing for long moments at a time and going away somewhere inside that head of his, but he was strong and good-looking. Kasha had pointed this out one night while the two of us folded laundry. "That man is the best lover in the universe," she'd said.

When another moan came from Granny's room, Jack moaned in response. He laid his head against my chest. "Oh, girl," he said, plenty loud enough for the others to hear.

"Stop it," I whispered.

"Ohhhh An-*nie,*" Jack said. He paused. When no sound came from them, he dropped his head back to my chest. His giggles shook my body.

What would an eavesdropper think if they overheard Jack and me having sex? That Jack got the best of it, definitely. He was always able to let go and enjoy it. I, on the other hand, held back. He was always having to ask what felt good, and this was because I was too ashamed to tell him what I wanted. Nice girls didn't do the things I did with him—that's what Granny had taught me. But what about Kasha? She'd been raised in the same house, yet she somehow had no reservations about what she should or shouldn't do.

Now that he and Kasha were in love again, D.W. had left Cincinnati and was renting a place in the north Georgia mountains. On a cold day in December, Kasha and D.W. went up to his place for a few days. D.W.'s truck broke down as he was driving Kasha home, so Jack and I went to fetch them. The four of us piled into Jack's truck and started back to D.W.'s place to drop him off, but it began to snow. Big flurries covered the windshield. We decided it'd be best to take D.W. home with us and then give him a ride back once the weather cleared.

On the drive home, the four of us sat bundled up and wedged together. Kasha's elbow kept digging into my ribs.

Jack pulled into a gas station parking lot.

Kasha said, "Let me out, babe. I need some hot chocolate or something."

D.W. opened the door, crawled out, then helped Kasha down. For about the hundredth time, I thought what an odd couple Kasha and D.W. made. She was thin and health-conscious, but D.W. wasn't the health-food type. He favored beer and red meat.

"I'll pay for gas," D.W. said. "Fill it up."

I slid off the seat behind Jack.

"Truck's warmer," Jack said, pointing back to the cab. He started the gas pump.

"I have to stretch my legs," I said and sidled up to him, laid my head against his chest.

A car pulled up to one of the pumps beside us, and a woman got out. She wore snow boots and a heavy puffer jacket. The woman watched me intently. I nodded at her but she didn't acknowledge me. Instead, she looked Jack up and down and then looked back at me. Instinctively, I took my head off his chest.

"It may not be about race. Maybe she envies you for being with a man as cute as me," Jack teased. When I looked up at him, he winked.

A Black woman and an Indian man is a rare pairing. I didn't like it when people stared, but it never bothered Jack.

Kasha and D.W. came out of the store. The woman at the pump still watched us. She huddled under the shelter of the carport. Ribbons of light snow fell behind her. Finally, she raised a hand and waved.

Kasha held two paper coffee cups. We all climbed into the truck, and Jack pulled out of the parking lot.

Kasha handed one of the cups to me, probably her way of saying thanks for making the trek to rescue her and D.W.

"What's this?" I asked, pointing at the lipstick stain around the cup's drinking hole. "You drank out of it?" I asked.

"How else was I supposed to know it was sweet enough?" she asked.

I handed the cup back to her.

"She was just trying to be nice," D.W. said. "And y'all are sisters. Swapping spit ain't a big deal."

"Maybe not to you. It grosses me out," I told him, pushing my head in front of Kasha's so that I could look him in the eye.

He gave me a go-to-hell look. "Everything bothers you. I never seen anybody so bothered," D.W. said. He scowled at me. It was evident he'd been holding it in for a while. This was the most D.W. had ever said to me at once.

Neither Jack nor Kasha said anything. It was the kind of silence that confirmed D.W.'s words. And yet his treatment of me felt foreign. When I was younger, I was the girl so often praised at church and at school. I made good grades and respected authority. Little Miss Perfect. That's how people tended to view me, and this was how I viewed myself. Sure, I judged others, but rarely had I seen this as a character flaw. D.W.'s words embarrassed and shamed me. I couldn't wait to get home and out of everyone's sight.

The snow slowed down a little, and Jack sped up, but we still moved along at only fifty miles an hour.

"We should be there by now," Kasha said. She held herself erect, tried not to lean into me when Jack rounded a curve. Her elbow dug into my ribs again.

"This is all your fault, Kasha," I said. "Why'd you have to drive off to the mountains during the worst weather of the year?"

"It wasn't snowing when we left!"

"Hey," Jack said. "Everybody calm down. Doesn't matter whose fault it is. We'll be home soon."

He'd hardly gotten the words out when the truck slid off the road. Everything moved in slow motion. Kasha screamed. I felt her elbow in my ribs again, heard D.W. draw in his breath. My bottom lifted off the seat and plopped down hard. When we stopped moving, I opened my eyes. We'd slid into a tree, and the truck's hood was dented.

In a shaky, stuttering voice I'd never heard before, Jack asked, "Everybody all right?" He let out a breath and put his hand on my thigh and squeezed it, then looked to the others, verifying we were all okay.

"I'm all right," Kasha said.

D.W. opened the door, went around and tried to pry open the truck's hood. Grunting and straining, he managed to raise it a few inches at a time. Kasha got out, drew her coat closer around herself, and stood by D.W. He fiddled with something under the hood.

"See if you can start it, Jack," D.W. said.

Jack stared off into the distance.

"Jack?" I said. "Are you hurt?" I shook his shoulder.

"I-I'm okay," he said. "Just shaken up." He gripped the steering wheel with his hands on three o'clock and nine o'clock.

"See if you can start it, Jack," D.W. said again.

Jack's hand shook as he reached out for the ignition switch. When he finally turned the key, the engine didn't say anything.

Kasha crawled back into the truck beside me. "Maybe someone will drive by and see us," she said.

D.W. came over to the driver's-side door.

"C'mon, man," he said to Jack, "let's walk up to the highway and flag down a car."

Jack didn't reply.

"I'll do it," I said to D.W.

Kasha let me out and then crawled back into the truck. D.W. took off his heavy overcoat and handed it to her. She draped it around herself.

The steep embankment was covered with snow, making the climb up to the main road a strenuous one. I slid down to the bottom twice. D.W. wasn't faring much better until he got the idea that we hold onto one another and use each other's weight to heft us up. When I slid for the third time, he dug in his heels and helped me right myself. With his other hand, he grabbed hold of a tree root that poked up from under the snow. Like a rock climber, he used the root to lift himself higher. I followed.

When we reached the top of the hill, I was breathing heavily and, despite the cold, sweating a little.

D.W. stopped to examine the truck's skid marks. "Good thing Jack was driving so careful," he said. "Otherwise we probably would've turned over, and we wouldn't have walked away from hitting that big old oak tree."

"Jack doesn't think so. He's probably blaming himself," I said.

"He's a good guy," D.W. said.

"He is," I said, suddenly wanting to run down the hill and tell him what a good guy he was.

"I bet you think I'm a monster," I said to D.W.

"A little," he said, and then chuckled. "I think your biggest problem with me is that you see only the teenage me." He shook his head. "No one stays who they were at seventeen. Everybody changes. I didn't always treat Kasha so good, but I'm better now. *We're* better now."

"This is the longest conversation I've had with you. When you come by the house, you barely even look at me."

"I walk on eggshells 'cause I don't want you to accuse me of stealing again."

His words nearly knocked the air out of me. "I'm sorry," I said. "I should—"

"You thought that since I argued with Kasha as a kid that I somehow turned into a thief?"

The way he put it made me feel like the dumbest person alive.

Headlights crested the hill. D.W. immediately started waving his arms. As the car braked, I turned to look down the hill at Jack's truck. He still sat there, his hands on the wheel. Kasha tugged on his coat sleeve, and the two of them got out and began to climb the hill toward us. As he placed his feet carefully on the snow, Jack met my eyes for a second and then looked down. Men like him think the world will cease spinning if they show vulnerability, but seeing it made me love him more. How many months had I gone now without telling him I loved him? Too many. I vowed to do it as soon as we were alone together.

Kasha and D.W. went over and talked with the driver that D.W. had flagged down. I took Jack's hand and squeezed it.

"Head doctor?" he asked.

I nodded. "Together," I said. "We'll figure it out."

You Can Have It

One night I get up and go stand in the living room doorway. The room is lit by only the TV screen and orange light from the kerosene heater. Kerosene fumes burn my eyes. Cold air brushes places my flannel nightgown doesn't cover—ankles, shins, and knees.

On the TV screen, the boxers move together for one moment. They hug each other, bare chest to bare chest. One man has his arms around the other man's waist, akin to a lovers' embrace. The man in the blue trunks cocks his head closer to his opponent's. Their bodies are slick with sweat, skins so damp and shiny they seem to have been rubbed down with body oil.

Mama's fingers dig into the plaid upholstery of her recliner. Not much ever excites my mama, but when she does get excited she holds her breath. I listen to her labored pants, want to poke her in the ribs and tell her to breathe.

A woman and two men sit on the couch. I recognize only one of them—Tim Reading, who was several years ahead of me in school when he dropped out. Though I haven't seen him in years, I haven't forgotten him. Tim sits calmly, chin angled down, shoulders and forehead pointed squarely at the TV. I look at his face, really study it—the high cheekbones and the wide, round nose. He has delicate lips. The light of the heater shows burn scars on the back of his neck. The story goes that Tim's mama was hopped up on drugs one night when she spilled a pan of hot cooking oil on him.

It is the year after I've finished high school, and Mama can't afford pay-per-view boxing matches on her own, so she invites her coworkers from the hatchery plant to watch the fights with her and chip in to pay for them. When she does this, they make such a commotion over the fights that I can't sleep. It's not quite eleven P.M. Though my parents are night owls, I'm the opposite.

A bell dings. The fighters withdraw from each other and shuffle into their corners. Trainers spurt water over the fighters and knead their massive shoulders.

My daddy walks through the living room carrying a basket of laundry. He looks at the screen, frowns, and shakes his head. "I wish y'all wouldn't watch that," Daddy says. "It's inhumane."

"No one makes them do it, sugar," Mama says, not taking her eyes off the screen. "They're fighters. It's what they do."

Daddy, his upper lip curled, looks around at the wadded-up napkins, beer bottles, and half-eaten platters of fried fish and hushpuppies on the coffee table and the floor. He puts the laundry basket down and begins to gather trash. "Gimme a hand, Macy," Daddy says to me.

I pick up three beer bottles sitting on the floor near my feet, scoop up some lipstick-stained napkins from the table and follow Daddy into the kitchen. We throw the mess into the trash bin and then head back into the living room.

Another bell dings on TV, signaling the boxers out of their corners. The man in the red trunks goes at the other guy. I admire his aggressiveness and physical strength. He backs the other man into a corner, beats the daylights out of him. The man in blue falls to the canvas.

Tim stands, casts a long shadow against the wall. He high-fives the woman on the couch and eagerly accepts bills from the man to his left.

I catch Tim's eye and smile. He smiles back.

I go to the high school football game on Friday night. There isn't much else to do here in Muscadine. Outside the stadium, all the extended-cab pickups are lined up along the outside of the chain-link fence, where the parking spots are longer. Popcorn makes the cold air salty. Cheerleaders shake their blue and white pompoms. One of my old basketball teammates, Ashley Crawley, waves for me to join her, though I just wave back and stay put. Being with the team feels so strange since our teammate Lucy drowned last year. Lucy and I were best friends, and we were the team's best players and the most likely to get scholarships. We'd planned to go to the same college. We were supposed to help each other because we didn't know what to expect from college. Our parents hadn't made it past high school.

I stare at the players on the field and then let my eyes sweep the stands. I'm not a football fan, but sometimes I come to the games to get out of the house and fight off the loneliness, and at other times I want to roll into that loneliness where no one can reach me. Lately, I've wanted to sleep more often than not. My friend Rachel says it's depression, but she's seen too many movies and thinks everyone is depressed. I think it's fear. Fear of leaving this town where my family has lived for so long, and fear of having to make new friends and new Friday-night plans.

At halftime, I leave the stadium, walk across the school parking lot to smoke a cigarette. The moon is very bright. Trumpets and trombones call out from the football field.

I've only been smoking for a few weeks, and I can only imagine what Lucy would've said about smoking and endurance and basketball. I put the cigarette butt in a trash bin.

As I'm heading back to the field, I see Tim walking on the other side of the parking lot. He turns right onto Curry Creek Road. My friend Rachel is my ride tonight, otherwise I'd offer him a ride. Where is he headed? I follow him down toward Curry Creek Bridge. The cicadas remind me of the low hum of voices from the football crowd. Tim moves through the tall grass, sending quiet brushing sounds across the field. Curiosity stops me from calling out to him. Better to see where he goes. I follow, pausing after every few steps to keep a good distance between us. The thigh-high grass leaves a clear path behind him as he moves farther from the road through a cluster of cedar trees.

Finally we come to the spot where the old McClure place used to be. The house was condemned years ago. Nothing remains there but an old toolshed that stands in what used to be the McClures' side yard. Weeds dominate the space. I close my eyes a second, not wanting to imagine the snakes and field rats that could be roaming the grass.

Tim opens the door to the shed and looks over his shoulder and right at me, or does he? It's dark out and I'm standing behind a tree, partially hidden. He stares in my direction for several seconds, and I know I've been found out.

"Saw you walking and wondered what you were up to. You staying here?"

Tim doesn't answer. Instead, he swings the book bag off his shoulder and lowers it to the ground.

I shiver and say, "It's cold out here," even though it isn't very cold. "Can I come in?"

Rather than answer me, he opens the shed's door. I follow him inside. The shed is so dark I can't see my feet. Tim rustles around on my left. A light switches on and then another. Flashlights. He sets them upright on the table by the handles so that the beams light the ceiling. Something scurries to my right. A spider. I hold my hand over my mouth. Spiders make me feel sick.

"Why ain't you in college?" he asks.

The question is unexpected. I keep watching the spider, hoping it will change direction and burrow under a shovel it has ambled past. Tim follows my line of sight, spots the spider, and steps on it. He moves his sneaker back and forth, grinding its body into the earth.

"I woulda gone if I was you," he says. "You could probably get a good job in an office someday, or somewhere like that."

I say, "How long have you been staying here?"

There is an air mattress in the middle of the floor. He sets his book bag down on top of it and doesn't answer me. I take off my jacket and lay it down on the mattress.

"Don't make yourself at home, girl. I don't like company out here."

I sit on the mattress, stare up at him.

“Quit playing, Macy.” He grabs my arm as if to pull me to my feet, but I dig my shoes into the ground and pull him toward me. He could easily snatch me up, but doesn’t. Instead, he flops down beside me on the mattress.

“I was sorry to hear about your mama,” I tell him.

Tim’s mama died last year. People said it was an overdose.

“Don’t you have any folks to stay with?” I ask.

“Got a cousin that works with your mama at the poultry, that’s how I heard about the pay-per-view party. I stay with my cousin most nights.”

“What about your folks in Spartanburg?”

“What you know about Spartanburg?” he asks.

“Heard you went over there to stay with family after you left high school.”

Tim stares at me a long time. My left knee is against his right one. I shift my body a little closer to his. He puts his mouth down by my ear, says, “What are you doing out here with me?”

The hardness of his face—the slashing cheekbones and strong nose—are softened by his lips. Those lips are pliant, almost too feminine for the rest of him. I run my pinky finger along his top lip’s upper ridge.

When Tim kisses my cheek, I close my eyes, feel the cold air and Tim’s cold fingertips on the inside of my thigh. I resist him, but only a little. I like his lips and hands on me, but I don’t like where we are. My fear of the spider comes back. It’s amplified by ten when I hear a scraping sound on the tin roof. I draw in my breath so fast that I start to cough. Tim says, “It’s just squirrels on the roof.” His cold fingers dig underneath my bra, find my breast, and squeeze a little too hard.

Aaron, my last boyfriend, was much more gentle than Tim. He held my head on his lap, stroked my hair, and told me I was beautiful. I rolled my eyes when he said it. I don’t like to be bullshitted. My looks are average, and boys only say otherwise when they are looking to get laid.

Something snakes its way across my ankle. I flinch. Tim leans down toward my feet and scoops something up. He flops down on his back, a green lizard in his hand. "This guy does that some nights. He likes to play around." Tim turns his head to me. His smile disappears as soon as he sees my face. He drops the lizard on the floor, and it scurries out of sight behind a cardboard box.

I try to let my expression soften, but I feel pukey again. "How can you live like this?" The words sound unintentionally disdainful.

"Look, girl, I'm always gonna live like this, or something like it. The question is, why is you out here with me?" Tim asks. He sits up and pushes his face closer to mine.

Energy radiates off his body and into mine. I know right then I'll keep coming back. Despite the spiders, lizards, and squirrels, staying away isn't an option. Being with him in the woods is better than hanging with Rachel these days, especially since she's just had a baby and is all the time complaining about her baby's daddy. Being with Tim is also better than sitting alone in my room and thinking about my life, how I'm nineteen years old and *should* have at least some plans for the future. But when I think of the future I see only a black, empty space.

"I like being here," I say, but the mood is ruined.

There's a hole in the ceiling. His angry face sits beside the moon.

"Are you sleeping here tonight?" I ask.

He doesn't answer. My denim jacket lies underneath his leg. He picks it up and tosses it toward the door.

I stand and put on the jacket before stepping out into the field. As I run through the grass and back toward Curry Creek Road, a memory passes through my mind. Back when I was about eight years old, I lost the coins Mama had given me for extra milk money. As I searched through my book bag on the school bus, Tim plopped down on the seat beside me.

"What are you hunting for?" he asked.

"My milk money. I lost it somewhere."

Tim reached into his pocket and held his hand out toward me. "Here," he said. His palm was pointed down and his fingers were curled into a loose fist. He dropped several quarters into my palm.

"You giving me this?" I asked him.

"Yeah," he said. "You can have it."

I go out to Tim's place again on Saturday, but he isn't there. On Sunday, just before dusk, I smell smoke as soon as I reach the grove of cedar trees leading up to the toolshed.

There's a small campfire going. Tim takes a long-handled cooking fork and rakes a package wrapped in tinfoil onto a plate. He opens the package, sniffs its contents.

"Whatcha got?" I ask.

He whips his head around to look at me.

"Scared?" I tease him.

He shrugs it off. "Not as scared as you. You scared of lizards, squirrels, maybe even your own shadow."

"And what are you scared of?" I ask.

"Dying," he says without any hesitation. He's sitting in front of the fire, looking up at me.

"You probably won't die for a long time," I tell him.

"Maybe, maybe not."

I sit beside him and he starts to eat the roasted chicken.

"Want to know what I'm scared of?" I ask.

He chews another bite of chicken, says, "I already know. You too obvious. You scared of failing. Scared to make friends better than me."

I roll my eyes at him.

He stops chewing, his hand halfway to his mouth. "You're just as good as those college kids," he says. "Better than most of 'em."

"I know that," I say.

"No you don't."

There are all types of intelligences. I wish Tim could see that being able to read people is a talent in itself, one that cannot be taught in a book. Tim is intuitive. But would he even know what that word means if I were to say it? I can't even explain it to him, not without gushing and embarrassing myself.

About a week later, I'm scanning the labels on cans of sweetcorn at work when I notice Mr. Klein, my boss, staring at something outside the store window. Mr. Klein is an older white man with glasses that always slide down his nose.

"Oh God," he mutters. "Here comes that Reading boy." Mr. Klein glances at me with his brow drawn before turning back to the window. "That boy's nothing but trouble. Last time he was in here he stole everything he could get his hands on."

I hear shouting outside, and I go over to the window, which is framed by icicles. We are in the midst of a rare ice storm. Our part of north Georgia doesn't get much ice or snow, but today ice covers everything—trees, roadway, pavement.

Out in the parking lot, Tim talks to a man in a blue sweatshirt. For a second I can't remember why the man looks so familiar, but then I recall his face from the night of the boxing match. He sat next to Tim that night; he was the one who lost the bet.

The man wears no coat or hat. He's pale with a bright red face, and I can't tell if he's red from the cold or because he's shouting at Tim. "Don't you ever—" the man says, but his words are drowned out by a semi on the highway.

Tim waves the man away and starts toward the store, but the man grabs Tim's elbow and presses his face into Tim's, his body upright, as if bracing for an attack. If they were animals, this would be the part where they bare their teeth.

Mr. Klein goes over to the counter, picks up the phone, and dials a number.

"Hey, this is Jim Klein. I'm calling to report that Tim Reading is out in front of my store," he says into the phone. He pauses for a moment and listens. "I made a police report last time and y'all didn't do nothin' about it. Just get a cop out here." He hangs up the phone and joins me at the window.

Tim shoves the man down onto the icy pavement.

Mr. Klein moves over to the door and yanks it open. He goes out and stands with his hands on his hips. "You can't come in here. I've already called the law. Just get on back where you come from." Mr. Klein looks at the man who stumbles as he gets to his feet. "Both of y'all. I don't want trouble."

But the man isn't listening or doesn't care. He walks up behind Tim and grabs him in a chokehold. I start to push past Mr. Klein in my hurry to get to Tim, but Mr. Klein grabs me. "Hey," he says. "You crazy? Stay in here." He pulls me back inside the store, slams the door shut, and latches the two deadbolts.

I follow Mr. Klein back to the window. Tim and the man wrestle on the ground. Tim climbs on top of him. I can't help but think that it looks like one partner mounting another in the bedroom. I half-expect to see Tim unzip his fly, but of course he doesn't. Instead, he draws back and punches the man square in the face. Before the man recovers, Tim punches him again. Blood spurts up into the air and lands on Tim's shoulder and on the pavement. Again and again I hear the sound of Tim's fist connecting with the man's face. It's like a sick beat to an enticing song. As sick as it makes me feel, I am intrigued by it. I cannot look away. I am mesmerized, even aroused, by watching a man try to kill another man.

My mind shifts to Tim's steady, forceful kisses. I feel their rhythm against my lips.

"Where're the damned cops?" Mr. Klein mutters. He dials numbers on the phone again.

"Yeah," he says. "Y'all better get down here. Tim's done jumped on Rodney Kilgore . . ."

We hear the police sirens and Mr. Klein looks out the window toward the police station.

I look to the left and the right, hoping to see a deputy's car, but they aren't here yet. I wonder how far away the sirens are as Tim climbs off of the bloody man. There is a moment when Tim stands there, looking over his shoulder, no doubt looking for the police car. He doesn't move, and for a moment I see him struggling with a choice. Act or do nothing? Move forward or stand still?

"He's beat the tar out of him. He's gon' need an ambulance . . . ," Mr. Klein says into the phone.

Tim runs across the railroad tracks and into the woods behind Northeast Georgia Bank. Mr. Klein slams down the phone.

A minute later, two police cars pull up to the gas pumps. An ambulance arrives, lights flashing. Two medics jump out. They lean over Kilgore's body as a deputy comes to talk with Mr. Klein. The deputy says his name is Lighthouse, but I know this already because I went to school with his daughter, Sybil Lighthouse. She has the same features—white-blond hair and impossibly white skin.

Mr. Klein explains what happened, how Tim pushed Kilgore and Kilgore tackled him.

"Did you see which way he went when he ran outta here?" Lighthouse asks.

"Up toward the woods," Mr. Klein says as I point in the opposite direction near the church.

"You think he went that way?" the officer asks me as he jerks his thumb over his shoulder.

"No," Mr. Klein says. "I saw him run behind the bank. Remember, Macy?"

"That's not what I saw," I say, pointing toward the church again. "While you were over there on the phone, he circled around and went back toward the church," I lie.

Officer Lighthouse looks back at Mr. Klein.

Mr. Klein shrugs. "She was in front of the window longer than I was. If she says it's so, then I reckon it is." My heart beats a little faster. I remember that moment when I tried to run out to help Tim and how Mr. Klein had pulled me back. Could he tell that I'd favored Tim? I stare into Mr. Klein's eyes a moment, and he squints at me. Dropping my eyes to the floor, I turn my back. I don't dare look at him again. He'd probably read my mind. Mr. Klein has known my family since forever; he used to fish with my granddaddy.

Lighthouse's police radio is clipped to his shoulder. He pushes a button on it and gives the dispatcher the info about Tim and the Baptist church. Then, he scribbles something on a pad.

After Lighthouse finishes with me, Mr. Klein says, "You can go on home now, Macy."

I walk to the stockroom to get my coat and purse. Out in the parking lot, I see that the ambulance has pulled out of the lot, but a small crowd of onlookers is still gathered by the gas pumps. As I crawl into my Chevy truck, Lighthouse comes up to me. He's watching me, and his eyebrows are drawn together.

A couple of years ago, Lighthouse was out directing traffic one day when my friend Kasha and I drove up to him. Lighthouse held up his hand for Kasha to stop the car, but Kasha ignored him and kept moving. Lighthouse blew his whistle and came hollering up the street.

Kasha was smoking a black and mild, which she had no business doing, since we were only sixteen. Lighthouse screamed and hollered with such authority that it scared Kasha. She slammed on brakes. Lighthouse came storming up toward the driver's side window. She panicked and put the lit cigar in the glovebox.

Lighthouse, face red, screamed, "I've seen y'all every morning speeding through town. When I'm out there in the street directing traffic, you stop!"

Kasha looked at me, eyes wide. She started to tear up. I smelled the cigar burning. We waited for him to give us a ticket, but he only glared at us. Finally, after standing there fuming for a full minute, he patted the car door roughly and told us to get the hell outta there.

As Lighthouse stands staring at me in Klein's parking lot, I wonder if he is remembering that day he yelled at Kasha and me. He knocks on the window, and I roll it down. He props himself up against the car, resting his elbows on the window ledge, blue veins visible through white skin.

"You know, Macy, my girl Sybil is at North Georgia College now. Thought you got a scholarship to somewhere?"

"Two offers," I tell him. "Wofford and Clemson."

"Those are good schools." He jerks his head back toward Klein's store. "But you decided to stay and work here instead?"

I'm more than sick of people telling me what I should be doing with my life.

"You and Tim are pretty good friends, aren't you?" he asks.

"Not really, sir."

"But you used to be?"

"His family knows my family, if that's what you mean. But until recently I haven't seen him around."

"That's 'cause he was locked up until recently. Was breaking into houses up in Spartanburg," he says.

My heart kicks up against my ribs, like a basketball thrown against a brick wall. I'd not heard anything about break-ins. He must be on parole now. Did that mean I'd broken some law by lying about which way he ran?

"I know you're a good kid, Macy. Stay away from that boy. If you see him, you call me." He reaches into his pocket and hands me a card with his name and the number to the sheriff's department on it.

Lighthouse stands back, and I maneuver my truck around the crowd. It's cold and the heater is busted, but I leave my window down anyway and let cold air in.

When I get to Curry Creek Bridge, I pull off the road and stop at the top of the embankment. For a moment, I sit there with the truck idling. I want to go looking for Tim in the shed, but I'm afraid to. What if Lighthouse finds me with Tim? The image of Tim on top of Kilgore comes back to me.

Maybe I can talk Tim into turning himself in. I open the door and get out of the truck. The grassy field isn't so scary in daylight. Before long, Tim's shed appears among the trees. At the window, I cup my hands around my eyes and peek inside. I can't see much of anything. I pause for a long moment to listen for movement.

Nothing.

When I get home, Mama is on our front porch.

"You all right?" She looks me up and down as though she expects to see a bullet hole.

"I'm fine."

I take my boots off and go into the kitchen. I sit by the window that looks out to our backyard.

Mama comes into the house and points to the blanket on the sofa.

"Did you know about that?" she asks me.

"Know about what?"

She grabs the blanket and brings it over to me. It is blue and has a seam loose on one corner.

"They found this in the camper," she says. She gestures to the little motor home in back of our house. "They think Tim's been squatting out there some nights. Tammy Randall saw him going in there. Did you know anything about it, Macy?"

"Of course not," I say, and it's the truth. I'm as shocked as she is. "You're the one who had him over here for your boxing party. If he's been in our camper, it's 'cause you did that." I turn from her and look out the window toward the woods.

Mama grabs my wrist and forces me around to look at her. "Do you know where he's run off to?" Mama asks me. "He's already got a warrant on him, Macy. If Kilgore dies, they'll bump it up to manslaughter. The cops explained it to me that way. If you know where he is, you better tell me," she says.

I look at the blanket slung over her shoulder.

"Answer me, girl," Mama says.

"No, I don't know anything about the blanket."

She shakes her head, and I can tell she doesn't believe me.

The next morning when I climb out of the shower, I hear Mama and Daddy talking in the kitchen.

"They got him last night," Daddy is saying. "I always did know that boy was something sour. His mama never could make him go to school. He was always off somewhere, racing four-wheelers, wild as the devil."

A rivulet of water runs down the side of my face and drips onto the towel. The rustling sound of a newspaper comes from the kitchen, and I imagine Daddy turning a page of the paper while he sips coffee. I slip on shorts and a tank top and go into the kitchen, hoping there's a story about Tim that I can read.

I nod good morning. Daddy starts another longwinded speech about how rotten he thinks Tim is. Mama nods her head in agreement. I roll my eyes when I think she isn't looking.

"What you rolling your eyes at, Miss Lady?" Mama asks.

"I hate how everyone thinks they know everything in hindsight. If you really knew he was so violent, you wouldn't have invited him over here," I say.

I lean over Mama to read the local paper. The story confirms what Daddy said, that Tim was apprehended the night before.

"Excuse you, ma'am," Mama says.

My wet hair has dripped onto her shirt sleeve. She snatches the paper up and snaps it shut.

"That boy always was wild," Daddy says again.

"He wasn't all bad. He—" I start, but then I stop when I notice Mama watching me.

"He *is* all bad," Daddy says. "He beat the stuffing out of Kilgore. They're saying Kilgore'll be out of work for weeks. He's got a family that depends on him."

"Kilgore's kids are crazy about him. Tim ain't got nobody," Mama says, looking pointedly at me.

"Everybody's got *some*body," I say.

I get a raise from Mr. Klein, enough money to rent a tiny apartment on Webster across from a laundry. The heat is busted those first few nights, and the train rumbles by at the most inconvenient times. My apartment is down the block from where Rachel lives with her baby, who is now preschool age. Time has flown by. When I think of high school, it seems a whole lifetime has passed. I've started some cosmetology classes at the junior college. This time next year, I'll be a hairdresser. Still, I can't help but wonder what I could've become as a student at Wofford College. I always imagine college girls to be white and formal and stuck-up. My junior college isn't Wofford, but it's good enough.

One night I walk down to visit Rachel. Nearly all the little houses have Christmas trees lit up in the windows and green and red wreaths on the front doors.

A man walks toward me. He wears a gray sweatshirt with the hood pulled over his head. He breaks his stride, looks sidelong at me, and crosses the street.

"Tim?" I say. He doesn't turn around, so I say it again, louder this time.

Tim walks faster, putting more and more distance between us.

I think about that day on the school bus when we were just kids, how he said, "You can have it." I think about his smooth skin, how it wasn't scarred yet. I remember the way his fingers brushed my palm when he slipped the coins to me.

June's Menorah

1959

My brother, Fitzgerald, came home carrying a brown paper bag. He held the top of the bag the way a person would hold the neck of a liquor bottle, fingers curled into a fist around it. Fitz didn't look left or right, just set one foot in front of the other in long, purposeful strides as he made his way to Papa's bedroom at the end of the hallway. He went in, left the door open behind himself. From my view at the end of the short hallway, I could see Papa on the bed. He lay the way I did whenever I felt sick—flat on his back with the covers pulled up to his chin—and when he made any movement of his head or arms he did it sluggishly, as if it pained him to move. A cigarette burned on the nightstand beside Papa; the smoke curled up around the top of his head. Fitz took the liquor from the paper sack and handed it to Papa. The bottle was covered with a black label. After a few of Papa's attempts at opening the bottle, Fitz took it from him, opened it, and handed it back. Papa drank several big gulps, then laid his head against the pillow and sighed as if the liquor were somehow medicinal. Papa mumbled something, and though I couldn't hear what he said, I heard Fitz's response, "I came back as soon as I could."

I whimpered. Fitz looked out into the hallway, saw me, and then stepped over and closed the door.

The springs in the settee shifted, and a second later Lisa, Fitz's girlfriend, came out of the living room and stood beside me in the hallway. "You all right, June?" she asked me.

I turned to face Lisa. Her black hair was parted down the middle and gathered at the nape of her neck. Long bangs brushed across her eyelids. Pretty Lisa was known as one of the sweetest teachers at my school.

I nodded at her.

She followed me back to the kitchen, and we sat down in ladder-back chairs.

Lisa wore a pink cotton dress with a row of white buttons shaped like carnations down the front. Her earrings were gold-colored balls. I never saw her in anything but a dress, and she knew how to apply makeup so that her eyes were accented and her cheeks were colored red, but not too bright. In contrast, Fitz had quit school in the eighth grade, and he always came home from his job at the cotton yard with sweat stains on his shirt and tufts of cotton stuck to his clothes and hair. I always did think Lisa and Fitz were an odd couple. She was constantly fussing over him—reminding him when he needed a shave, clipping his fingernails, ironing his pants.

I picked up *Anne Frank: The Diary of a Young Girl.* Lisa had given me the book the day before, and I was transfixed by it. Anne was holed up in an attic, oppressed by the Nazi regime; I often felt trapped in our house, oppressed by my papa's glassy eyes. I felt a kinship with Anne. I stared at her photo on the cover of the book until I felt Lisa's eyes on me. She sat grinning as she watched me, and I could tell Lisa felt good about giving me a present I loved.

I heard Papa's bedroom door open, and then the sound of Fitz's footsteps making their way toward us on the hardwood floor of the hallway. Fitz's walk—heavy enough to move the boards of our old house and quick enough to remind me of how limber he was—was just as distinguishable as his laugh. His laugh was more of a guffaw, a cross between a cough and a yell. I missed the sound of that laugh. Fitz had been so preoccupied with tending to Papa that there seemed to be no laughter left in him.

Fitz was ten years older than me, which would've made him only twenty-five, and yet already his hair was going gray around his temple. The gray hair and the large belly that hung over his belt made him look older than his years.

"Let's sit outside a while," he said.

I grabbed my book and followed the two of them out onto our porch. Having a book close at hand always made me feel comforted.

Our neighbors, the Grangers, had their smokehouse door open, and the wind carried the smell of smoked pork to us. Mr. Ted Granger stood in his yard with his two old dogs. When he saw us come out to the porch, he threw up a hand in greeting and then disappeared into the smokehouse. December had come, but it was unseasonably warm. Though the trees were bare and gray, sunlight hung over everything, and that day felt like early springtime.

"Junie," Fitz said to me.

I looked over to where he sat beside Lisa on the wicker loveseat. Both of them were looking at me.

"What is it?" I asked.

"We're getting married," Fitz said.

I looked out across the field at the Grangers's house. When I cut my eyes back to them, their smiles were fading.

"I'll go make us some coffee," Lisa said and went into the house.

Fitz said, "Lisa's a good woman. She's helped me through some hard times . . ."

"I never said I don't like Lisa. I think she's nice."

"Then why don't you want me to marry her?"

"I never said that."

"You don't gotta say it. You've got your lips all drawn in."

I pushed my lips back out. "There," I said, gesturing at my mouth. "Better?"

"I love Lisa, and she loves me. And she thinks a lot of you, Junie."

He and Lisa had been going together since the year before, when she moved to Muscadine from a colored college in Savannah. And he was right—Lisa treated me well. She was always bringing me books to read, and on my birthday she had given me a pair of pearl earrings.

Fitz and I sat in silence. Somewhere in the distance, a rooster crowed. Probably one of Hoyt Tinsley's birds. They liked to crow at all times of the day and night. I looked out at our yard. A wide stretch of brown grass ran back toward a thicket of pine trees. The beginning of our walking path peeked out between the trees. The path had been worn down to mostly dirt. Muscadine and honeysuckle vines lined each side of the path, and it was a short walk down that path to reach our well and outhouse. If you continued for a few miles past the outhouse, you would run straight into the back door of the post office in Muscadine.

My daddy's daddy had bought these acres long before Fitz and I were born. Granddaddy had come from a big sharecropping family, and he and his brothers and sisters saved for years to buy three plots of land around the county. My granddaddy shared this house with one of his brothers. Ever since I could remember, I heard stories about the brothers raising two families in this white clapboard of ours.

When I finally looked over at Fitz again, he was staring at me.

"It's just that things will change so much when you get married. You're barely around the house as it is anymore," I said.

"I won't be leaving. She'll move in with us." He fiddled with one of the big, brown buttons on his shirt, twisted it around and around. The button came off in his hand. "Dang it," he said, frowning down at his abdomen. His shirt gaped open, and I could see his white undershirt.

I'll sew it back on, honey," Lisa said as she came through the screen door. She came out onto the porch with the coffee as Fitz slipped out of his shirt. He sat back in his chair, said, "Ted Granger came over yesterday, gave us some pork."

"That was nice of him," Lisa said.

"Guess he feels sorry for us, with Daniel being as sick as he is."

Lisa said, "We could plow up the back field and plant some crops. People in town'll pay for beans and corn and okra next summer and fall."

"I'm not too worried about money. We'll eat," Fitz told her. "But Daniel's not getting any better. I've 'bout gave up on him."

Fitz always called Papa by his first name, Daniel. I think it was Fitz's way of showing his disrespect.

"Well, you don't have to worry about me eating any of that pork," I said. "It's not kosher. I just decided I won't eat hogs anymore."

"Kosher?" Fitz asked.

"Jewish people don't eat certain foods," Lisa explained to him.

"Jewish people? What's that got to do with us? You're a colored girl, Junie."

"I'm reading Anne Frank's diary. Anne was a famous Jew," I told him.

I handed the diary to Fitz, tried to entice him into reading it, even gave him a synopsis.

"*What?*" he asked. "You mean she *dies* at the end, June?"

"Yeah," I said.

He shook his head at me. "As if things ain't bad enough, you over here reading the saddest shit you can find."

"June!" Papa called to me from his bedroom. "June, come in here."

Though Papa was hollering for me, it was Fitz who jumped up. He started toward the short hallway and looked expectantly over his shoulder at me. I didn't want to go in there, but I let out the breath I'd been holding and followed Fitz anyway. Fitz moved a lot like our father used to—quick and surefooted with one shoulder higher than the other. Just as Fitz reached for the doorknob, I took hold of his elbow.

"I don't wanna go in," I whispered.

"I know you don't like seeing him like this, but he'll probably look better and better the longer I wean him off the stuff. He just needs some time to dry out, that's all."

Dry out. I never understood that phrase. Papa wasn't wet, not even damp. He was just a drinking man who couldn't keep a job, couldn't be a decent father.

For a moment, I wished our mama was still alive. She had died when I was four. I barely remembered her at all, and I usually only missed her when I felt scared or lonely. A memory came to mind: *I am standing beside Fitz. Black crows peck the ground. I'm wearing a white dress, and everyone is crying. I want to see Mama, but I can't. She's in the big hole in the ground.*

Papa's door squeaked as Fitz opened it and went inside.

I turned away, intending to head back out to the porch for some fresh air, but Lisa had settled herself down at the kitchen table and was sewing the button on Fitz's shirt. Lisa fidgeted with the button, loosening the tension against the fabric, but her eyes were on me. She was using my mama's old sewing kit—a small aluminum tin filled with half a dozen different colors of thread. Assorted buttons lined the bottom of the tin.

"That was my mama's," I said.

Her hand stopped in midair as she pulled a piece of thread through Fitz's button. "Is it a keepsake?" she asked.

She looked as if she didn't know what to do, then she snipped the thread from the spool, slipped the little scissors back into the kit, and gently closed the lid.

"Here," she said, holding the kit out to me. "I'm sorry. I won't use it again." Her voice sounded irritated, but when I met her eyes, she smiled. I felt my own lips soften into a smile. When Lisa smiled like that, she reminded me of a picture I had of Mama. Both Mama and Lisa had straight teeth, big cheek apples, and wide eyes like those seen on a deer or a bunny rabbit or some other gentle animal.

I didn't take the sewing kit from her. Instead, I turned and went out onto the porch again.

It bothered me that Lisa was so comfortable in our house already, that she had found Mama's kit in the kitchen drawer and was making Fitz's coffee. But mostly, I was upset that she was marrying my brother. I was used to a life with just Fitz and Papa, and I didn't want to share Fitz with anyone.

I reread several pages of Anne's diary and then closed the book. Staring out into our backyard, I thought of Anne and her parents. She was close to her father but thought her mother didn't understand her. Would Mama and I have been close if she had lived? Sometimes I asked Fitz about her. He told me she used to hold my hand and lead me around her flower garden, naming each plant and flower as she pointed to it. *Petunia. Elephant's Ear. Daylily. Daisy.*

Fitz came out to the porch carrying a coffee mug.

"He just wanted to talk to you, that's all," Fitz said. "I think he gets lonesome in there. And he wanted the window open. His lungs is still not clear yet. I'm trying to get him to stop smoking that old pipe, but he's not hearing me."

Papa had been coughing raucously for several months. At night, I'd lie in bed and listen to him carry on as if he couldn't catch his breath. At first Fitz had thought it was pneumonia, but I had had pneumonia once when I was about eight or nine years old and it hadn't lasted that long. Fitz had taken Papa to Dr. Creighton, who said it was a lung sickness.

There were tears forming in Fitz's eyes. I had never seen him cry and couldn't bear the thought of seeing it just then.

I turned my face from him and said, "I think I want to learn Yiddish. Anne Frank spoke German and Dutch, and I'm not sure if she spoke Yiddish, but Y-Yiddish is still sp-spoken by Jews everywhere," I said, hating that I kept stammering.

I didn't tell him that I was also considering having everyone call me by my middle name: Anne. Or maybe Annie. Annie Crawley.

Lisa came out of the house and went to the porch steps. Behind her, the screen door slammed shut. She carried a patent-leather handbag with a red floral scarf tied around the handle. "Ready to go, honey?" she asked, latching her purse.

Lisa boarded down the road from us with Ms. Corrina Atkinson, and Fitz always walked her home in the evenings when she came to visit.

Fitz put the mug on the wicker table and joined her at the steps. The sun was low in the sky, and its light caught the side of Lisa's face and the back of her braid.

The two of them descended the steps side by side, and I watched their silhouettes until they passed the sweet gum tree at the fork in the road.

Lisa taught the eleventh grade, and I was in the tenth grade classroom down the hallway from her. My teacher was Miss Ruby Finch, and one morning just before Miss Finch stood to address the class, Lisa came in to talk with her. Lisa held out her hand to show off the little sterling silver engagement ring that had belonged to my mama. Miss Finch, a woman whom I had never heard gush, spread Lisa's hand over her own hand as she stared, wide-eyed, at the ring. Miss Finch oohed and ahhed. She hugged Lisa so enthusiastically that they both almost toppled over.

After we were dismissed for noon dinner, I noticed that Lisa had left her red coffee cup on Miss Finch's desk. I was the last one out of the room, and when I went past the desk I picked up the cup. By the time I walked out of the schoolhouse most of the other kids had gathered in the yard or were headed home to eat. I ducked around the back of the school and went down to the outhouse, opened the door, and tossed the cup into the shit hole.

That afternoon, nosy Emma Granger found it and told Miss Finch. Only Emma would be enough of a busybody to look down the hole while using the outhouse.

Miss Finch was a stern woman who could be a tyrant when she got upset. She kept a wooden paddle in her top left drawer, and even though we were all too old to be paddled she used it several times a week on students who were boisterous, failed to keep up with reading lessons, or did anything that might be considered distracting.

Miss Finch narrowed her eyes at us and walked around the room. I was sitting in front next to the coal heater, and the heat of the furnace began to feel especially hot on me. I undid the button of my Peter Pan collar and fanned my face with one hand.

"Maybe we can rinse the cup out," said Jerry Addams. He stood up. "I'll go get some water and soap. Where's that cup at?"

"I left it in the crapper, Jerry," Emma said. "And ew, you nasty. Don't nobody wanna drink outta no doo-doo cup."

"Sit down, Jerry," Miss Finch said and then gave a long pause before adding, "If no one will admit to it, I'll have to paddle all of you."

She folded her arms in front of her chest. No one said anything.

Miss Finch walked over to her desk, opened the top left drawer, and took out the paddle.

"Jerry, we'll start with you. Come on up here."

Jerry stood again, but instead of walking toward Miss Finch, he said, "Ever who did it, just say you did it. I ain't about to get paddled over something I didn't do."

Heels clicked across the hardwood floor of the hallway, and a second later Lisa stood in the doorway. She pushed up the sleeves of her gray wool dress.

"Miss Ruby," Lisa said, "I know who took my cup . . ."

I bit my thumbnail, tasted blood.

". . . and I'll discipline that person privately," Lisa said.

I was grateful to Lisa. I was even more grateful when two days later in our kitchen Fitz asked her, "Where's that cup you always drink out of?"

I turned and looked at Lisa so quickly that I must've given myself away. If she had had any doubt that I'd taken her cup, it diminished. We looked at each other for several heartbeats, and then, to my surprise, she said, "I must've left it at the school."

I was surprised yet again when I came in from the creek that weekend to find a gold-colored menorah sitting on the end table next to the Christmas tree. I had never actually seen a menorah in real life, only in pictures. Our menorah shone so much that it looked to have been polished. The nine candleholders held one long, thin candle apiece.

Our family was Baptist, and I had been to church and Sunday school nearly every Sunday that I could remember. Though I never, ever felt the presence of any sort of god in our church services, I sang the songs and bowed my head in prayer. I sometimes felt guilty when people talked about God. I felt guilty for not believing.

On the day of my first communion, I did not want to believe that the cracker and the grape juice were the actual body and blood of Christ. I was terrified. Fitz had to comfort me after I bit into the wafer, made a gagging noise, and spat it out on his lap.

Somehow, I thought that reading the Torah and praying as a Jew would make me feel different or *right*. The Christian god had not worked for me, so I tested out the Jewish one, even though my knowledge of Judaism was very limited. The only Jew I knew was Nathan Siegler, a man who owned the department store in town. I ordered both a Torah and a Yiddish/English dictionary from him. Fitz thought I had flown the coop for spending part of my sewing money on such things, but as soon as the package came in I ran all the way home from town with it and took it down to the creek at the edge of our property line. I sat in the grass and read the first pages of the Torah. I was disappointed that the words did not have any big or significant meaning to me. Reading it made me feel no different than when I read the Bible.

I perused the Yiddish dictionary, memorized words and pronunciations in Yiddish. I even imagined conversations in which I could use Yiddish words. "Yes, Mr. Siegler," I would say the next time I was in town, "I hate to schlep in here like this, but I've been mighty tired lately. Isn't that a mishegoss? Fifteen years old and schlepping around like some old person!"

I practiced these dialogues again and again, though I knew I could never realistically use them. Colored folks didn't even look white folks in the eyes, not even the Jewish ones, and so the idea of me having a real conversation with Mr. Siegler was absurd.

And when I was down at the creek studying my dictionary, my mind was often too preoccupied to focus on what I was reading. I was distracted by thoughts of Fitz marrying Lisa and moving into his own house, despite that he had told me he wouldn't leave. The thought of being left alone in that house with Papa scared me most. What if he were to get really sick and die while I was there alone with him?

When I thought of these things, I put down the dictionary and screamed as long and as loud as I could. I scared the squirrels in their trees. I sent a large buck bounding off in the opposite direction. My face grew sore from forcing my jowls open. My lungs begged for relief.

Lisa began to spend more time at our house. In the afternoons before Fitz came home, she swept the floor or scrubbed laundry or cleaned the house in some other way. Usually around five o'clock, she and I made dinner together. Using the pork Mr. Granger had given us, we made ground sausage, turnip greens seasoned with bacon fat, and Brunswick stew.

I went back on my vow to quit eating pork.

When Lisa and I would see Fitz's headlights through the living room curtains at quarter after six, we would get up and go to the front door to meet him. As soon as Fitz walked in, Lisa took his coat off and hung it on the rack by the door, then she unlaced his boots and carried them into the laundry room and sprinkled baking soda in them. When she came back into the living room, she sat beside him on the settee and rested her head against his shoulder.

One time she winked at me and gestured at Fitz and said, "I love that man," as if she needed to announce it.

I never saw Fitz as happy as he was on those evenings. They'd sit for a while and talk, and then Fitz would sigh and put together a plate to carry in to Papa's room.

The Diary of Anne Frank came out that year, and I begged Fitz to carry me to the picture show in Athens to see it. In the end, Lisa rode along with us in Papa's old Packard.

When we got to the theater, the white section down front was half-full, but the three of us were the only ones seated in the colored balcony.

"I wish we could sit closer to the screen," I said as I looked down at the white section.

"I think we've got the best seats in the house. We've got the whole balcony to ourselves," Lisa said as she gestured around us at the empty seats.

"Shhh," I said.

As the movie started, I could feel my heart beat a little faster. Everything seemed so clear on that big screen. The music was sad, loud, and full. The actors, brilliant and eloquent. Millie Perkins, with her sweet smile and her bangs skimming across her eyelids, was the one I'd always remember. She was Anne, the girl I wanted to befriend.

Lisa said something to Fitz. I shushed her.

On the screen, Anne cried for Pim to come to her room and speak with her.

Lisa whispered again. Though I couldn't hear what she said and could barely hear her voice, I shushed her.

On the screen, Anne handed out Hanukkah presents to everyone—an erased crossword puzzle for Margot, a ball of yarn for the cat, a razor for Peter.

A minute later I shushed Lisa even when she wasn't speaking.

Fitz was sitting between us. He took hold of my wrist, brought his face an inch from my cheek, and said, "Stop it."

I stood, went down the aisle and out into the hallway, and found the sunlight too bright on my face.

That December day was especially warm. I sat in the Packard and waited for Fitz to come comfort me.

Five minutes went by, then ten, twenty.

When he finally did come out, it was dusk. He slid onto the driver's seat and motioned for me to get in back.

"No," I said. "I wanna ride in front."

He sighed. "June, get in the back."

"She rode in front all the way up here. It's my turn," I said.

"I don't mind the back seat," Lisa said.

"Well, I *do* mind," he said.

I stared at Fitz. He stared back. I crossed my arms. He got out of the car, rounded the hood, and opened the front passenger door. He pulled me gently from the car.

"Ow!" I overreacted as if he'd hit me.

"Fitz, don't hurt her."

"I'm not hurting her," he said, but he let go of my arm anyway. Fitz turned to walk back toward the driver's side as he grumbled to Lisa, "You've got to stop babying her. She needs to learn she can't always have her way." He looked at me and said, "You've got three seconds to get your little ass in the back seat."

I looked back and forth between the two of them, not sure what I expected to happen.

Fitz smacked his hand on the driver's side door. He narrowed his eyes at me.

I opened the back door and crawled in.

We drove toward home with the windows down and Fitz's left elbow jutting out the window. I seethed in the back seat, glared at the backs of their heads, even though I knew how unfair I was being. Lisa had always been kind to me.

As we drove, the smell of grass and pine trees wafted in through the open windows. Every so often, I'd spot a pair of fluorescent night eyes glowing beneath those giant trees or standing still by the roadside.

At the house, I went in and lay down with my face under the Christmas tree, a tall fir with blue and silver tinsel, and stared up at the lights. The menorah still sat on the end table. I had touched it many times by then, had run my fingers over the bright metal and imagined it lit and glowing, but I hadn't brought myself to light it. To do so would be to accept the person who had given it.

Fitz and Lisa talked together on the back porch. My ears pricked up when I heard my name.

"You have to be more firm with June," Fitz said. "She needs to start respecting you the way she does me and Daniel."

"I think she needs to get used to me first. And I could never be too hard on her," Lisa said. "I just love her. She's so quiet and observant."

I had thought Lisa was nice to me so that she could gain favor with Fitz. It was surprising to hear her say she loved me. Did she?

After a moment, I didn't hear their voices anymore. I got up and went to the screen door in the kitchen. The moon was bright, but I could barely make out their two figures. They stood under a clump of pine trees. His hands were on her shoulders. His red shirt lay on the ground. They were kissing.

Papa's voice called, "Fitz? June?"

I stood there for a long moment, half-expecting to see Fitz come through the door and move down the hallway toward Papa's room.

"June? Fitz?" he said again, his voice raspy. He was short of breath. He was always short of breath.

Fitz pulled Lisa into the canopy of trees. The tail of her yellow skirt disappeared behind them.

I wanted to call out to Fitz and Lisa, to beg them not to leave me.

"Fitz. Come in here," Papa called insistently.

As I moved toward Papa's room, I could hear my own breathing. When I got to the door, I hesitated. I wished there was a button to mash to slow my heart rate.

The bedsprings shifted, and then something bumped against the floor. Thinking that he had fallen, I twisted the knob and pushed open the door.

The curtains were open and a shaft of moonlight reflected off Papa's dresser mirror. He reclined against his headboard. His wooden cane lay on the floor, and I guessed that it had fallen and made the bumping noise.

"Fitz?" he said.

"It's me, Papa. It's Junie."

I stepped into the room.

"It's 'bout time," he said. "Where you been these weeks?"

I didn't say anything, and I worried he'd ask me again. What could I say?

I sat down in the chair near the headboard. We looked at one another through the hazy light cast by the oil lamp on the dresser. He was so thin that the long, flat shape of him beneath the blankets seemed to be a trick of the light. I blinked and rubbed my eyes.

"How you doing in school, Junie? Still reading those books?"

I nodded.

"That's good," he said.

I thought he winked at me, but maybe he was just drowsy.

"I want you to come in to see me sometimes," he said. "It'll be easier for you when I pass, easier to accept it." He coughed and then said, "You strong. You be all right when I go."

It was the first time any of us had mentioned that he would die. We'd all thought about it, I was sure of that, but no one had used the word.

His eyes closed. The nightmare where Papa dies in front of me while I'm in the house alone came to mind. I stood up and shook his arm.

"Papa?!"

His eyes opened and his mouth made a perfect *O*.

"What is it?" he asked.

"Are you okay?"

He flicked out his tongue to wet his parched lips. "Yeah, I feel about like I usually do. Sleepy though."

His eyes closed again. I watched him sleep.

The kitchen door opened, and Fitz and Lisa talked in quiet voices.

"June?" Fitz called. "You in the bed already? I'm about to carry Lisa home now, okay?"

I heard him walk down the hallway and pause outside my room as though he were talking to me through the door.

"I'm in here," I called to him.

Fitz came down the hallway and stood just inside the doorway. "You finally came in here. It ain't so bad, see?" he said.

"He was calling for us," I said.

"Why didn't you call me? I was just outside."

I said the first thing that came to mind: "I didn't think you could get your clothes back on fast enough."

Fitz's mouth fell open.

Papa made a sound, and at first I thought it was a cough. When I looked at him, I saw the grin on his face. His shoulders shook with laughter.

"Said you caught him with his pants down, baby girl?" Papa wheezed.

Fitz joined in. I didn't think it was very funny, but hearing them laugh together was enough to make me smile.

"What is it?" Lisa asked, coming down the hallway.

Fitz repeated the joke to her. Lisa looked over at me. She covered her smile with her hand.

Fitz sat down in the recliner and Lisa went over and half-perched against the arm of it.

I stood for a moment and listened to the three of them talk about the Grangers' farm and Lisa and Fitz's plans to sow seeds in the springtime.

I went to the living room and took the menorah from the cold tabletop and carried it back to my room. I set it down on my nightstand, and then I lay on top of my bedcovers. Though I left the menorah unlit, the brass shone in one corner of my room.

The Sense of Touch

My husband had been dead for nearly a year when the quarantine started. His death had left me all alone in our apartment, and then the pandemic hit and I felt all alone in the world. My neighbor, Robin, and her baby were the only two people I had regular contact with face-to-face. Robin said I needed to start dating again, but how do you date in the middle of a pandemic? I tried the online thing, did a few virtual dates. I found several men to sext with. Some of them wanted to use FaceTime or Skype. I declined. Nonnegotiable. It was the texting and the voice calls, or else it was nothing. For the remainder of that spring and into the summer, I followed a nightly routine. First, I'd wash my dinner plate and glass. Then, I'd return one or two of the guys' texts. Finally, I'd put in my earbuds and chat with one for a while.

Two called me regularly. One was a fiftyish white guy who said he was Minnesotan. He got off on chatting with me because I'm Black. He first said he was married, though I eventually doubted that because he always volunteered lame excuses for why the wife was out of town. (There were only so many weeks she could *possibly* be visiting family.) He thought I was petite, though I'm nearly six foot tall. I also told him I'm dark-skinned, though I'm actually quite light, and because he asked me that first night, "How small are your boobs?" I knew he wanted them small, so I deducted a couple of cup sizes. He said he's

Norwegian, and he once bragged about his blond hair and blue eyes. I've never favored those features.

"I love Black girls," the Norwegian Minnesotan said. "I been with Black girls. My last girl was Black."

I rolled my eyes. Most of the white guys who talked to me eventually said something like, "I've never been with a Black girl" or "I heard Black girls give the best head."

Pretty soon, my conversations with the Norwegian Minnesotan grew tiresome. He asked to tie me up, grunted like a sow for about three minutes while asking me to reaffirm how good he made me feel, how big he was, and how I was his bad girl who needed pounding. There were so many guys like him. Too many to count, *really.*

The other guy who called me regularly was Anthony, a thirty-something-year-old, like me. He traveled a lot for work and would call from various hotel rooms. Once he put me on hold for a minute, during which I heard a woman saying something like, "Hi, Mr. Ventura. You'll be in room 402." Then she called for a man to help him with his bags. All of those little details made me believe pretty much everything this guy said.

Anthony did everyday things when we chatted. Sometimes I heard the TV in the background. Chewing. The tab on a can of Coke popping open. He just had Ethiopian food for the first time. He's shocked by the level of violence in a new HBO show he's watching. I liked our conversations. He never wanted me to pretend. When we first started talking, I felt so instantly comfortable with him that when he asked what I had on, I told him the truth: Pink cotton shorts and a white tank top. "Any bra or panties?" he asked.

"Nope."

"Sweet."

He said he was from New York City, and I could hear the city in his voice, that distinct way of pronouncing his *A* sounds. He also used both double and triple negatives, said things like, "Ain't never got no," which made me judge him as uneducated, though he'd attended an Ivy League business school. He was sexier than the Norwegian Minnesotan, and he had this loud, spontaneous laugh—ha! ha! ha!—that endeared him to me. Anthony called me "sweetheart," but because he omitted the *R* it sounded like *sweethot.*

Whenever I answered his calls, Anthony was breathless, like he was right at the brink. It amazed me how he could be at the brink for ten minutes, finish, and then chat for five minutes and be suddenly at the brink again. I imagined he had a penis he could pump up at will. Like a blowup doll.

One night, he hung around after he'd finished. "What'd you do today, sweethot?" he asked. I could hear water running, and I imagined him washing himself off at the sink.

"Just another day in quarantine," I told him.

He chuckled. "I'm so sick of this shit. Atlanta ain't New York, but at least I'd have stuff to do if I wasn't quarantined."

"Atlanta?" I said. I'd thought he lived out of state, which was one reason I'd chosen to chat with him on the dating site.

"Yeh. I'm in Atlanta now," he said. "Moved here a couple weeks ago. Business is slow 'cause of all this COVID stuff. Where do you live?" he asked.

"Muscadine," I said.

"Ah, okay. Never heard of that. I'm in Cobb County." He sighed and I imagined him sinking into the cushions of his couch. "Do you go out for groceries?" he asked. "With your little mask on?" he said and tittered. In a quieter voice, he said, "You ever meet up with guys from the site?"

"Well," I said, drawing the word out as I searched for an answer. The truth was, of course, that I'd never met anyone from the site and never wanted to. Half the guys who contacted me were creepy. The other half, the ones who just seemed like ordinary guys suffering loneliness, didn't interest me. Plus, I didn't think it responsible to go on any unnecessary outings during a pandemic.

"No," I said. "Sounds like a good way to catch corona, or get your liver eaten with some fava beans and Chianti."

He gave me that ha! ha! ha! laugh and gasped out: "*Silence of the Lambs*. I love that movie. What else you watch?"

"Eighties teen movies. I used to watch those with my husband . . . ," I said, my voice trailing off.

"Alyssa? You there?"

"Yes," I said quietly. "I'm here."

"So you're married?"

"I'm not married."

"You just said *husband*," he said, his voice sharp on the last word.

I let out an annoyed sigh. "Yeah," I said. "I was married. He passed away."

He went quiet a few seconds. "Sorry to hear that," he said.

After that, we went several nights without talking. I assumed he was either busy or found someone else.

Around March of that year, three of my coworkers at the plastics factory got sick. The company did two big layoffs in March and April and put the rest of us on furlough until, as our supervisor said, "Only God knows when."

After the plant shut down, I had too much time on my hands. I watched movies. I learned how to cornrow after watching half a dozen YouTube videos. For one long afternoon, I practiced on myself, sitting on a barstool in front of the bathroom mirror and pulling my hair tight against my scalp. Then, I stood on the back porch and looked out to the park. It was nearly empty, just as it had been for weeks. I liked to admire crowds, but only from a distance. When amidst one, I felt nervous, like I couldn't breathe. From my back porch, I could keep a good fifty yards from the park and still enjoy the squeals of young kids laughing as they ran or swung. The park was never full in those days, though, and delightful squeals were nonexistent.

Every day, there was more talk of the virus. New symptoms. A growing number of both deaths and confirmed positive cases. Somewhere, after days of living in isolation, a man killed himself.

"You have a boyfriend over there?" Anthony asked the next time he called.

"Why?"

"'Cause when I meet you in person, I don't want nobody else in the way."

I smiled. A genuine smile. This rarely happened while on the phone with a guy. Usually I smiled outwardly as a way of putting cheeriness in my voice. Fake.

"Boyfriend or no?"

"No boyfriend," I said, realizing that I did want to meet him. My curiosity was getting the better of me.

"Good. As I said before, no woman here. No kids. You could come over anytime. Be as loud as you want. We could do—ha! ha! ha!—whatever."

I peeled off my socks and threw them toward the laundry hamper. "Is Anthony your real name?"

"Sure is, sweethot," he said. "Text me anytime you want. I don't like things so one-sided, with me calling you every time. Just text, Alyssa. I know you would like me," he said, his voice oozing confidence.

A short silence followed, and I worried he'd hung up.

"Anthony?"

"I'm here," he said, and then, "Tell me how your husband died."

I swallowed.

"Tell me."

A dull ache began to form in my temple. "A work accident in a factory," I said, rubbing my head.

"I'm so sorry, baby," he said.

There was a scraping noise on the front porch, like someone or something bumping up against the chair out there.

I drew in a quick breath, and Anthony asked, "What is it?"

I whispered, "I think someone's on my porch."

The clock on my cell phone said 10:48.

"Go to the door and check," he said.

I took a deep breath and went out into the hall.

At the front door, I switched on the porch light and peeked through the blinds. The clay pot lay on its side, cracked in half, the geranium and a gob of dirt spilled out on the porch slats.

"See anything?" Anthony asked, and I startled at the sound of his voice.

"Someone knocked over the plant I keep outside."

"Probably just the wind. Is it gusting?"

I listened for my wind chimes but heard nothing. I summoned my courage, opened the front door, and glimpsed a man's retreating figure moving into the shadows. It was my husband. I blinked and squinted to no avail. He was gone in a split second, but the streetlight had illuminated his wide shoulders, the dark brown skin of his bald head, and the red-and-black flannel jacket my husband had often worn.

"Everything good?" Anthony asked.

"No," I croaked out. I closed the door and fastened both locks. "I saw someone walking away from my porch."

"Call the cops," he said. "They can patrol your neighborhood more, keep people like that away." There was a pause on the line and then he said, "Are you okay? Shaken up?"

I walked back to my bedroom, my heart beating faster than usual, and I realized I was breathing heavily.

"Baby," he said. "I'm here. I want you to keep me on the line with you until you're comfortable enough to sleep."

"That's not necessary—"

"Do it," he said.

I pulled open the bedroom closet door and pushed hangers left and right as I searched for my husband's flannel jacket. There. There it was, pushed all the way over to the left-hand side of the closet rod. I pulled the red-and-black jacket from its hanger, clumsily unbuttoned it, and pulled it on over my tank top. I climbed into bed and lay on my side. One earbud began to make my ear sore, so I disconnected the earbuds, tossed them on the dresser, and put Anthony on speaker phone. I hugged myself. When my husband was here, he'd lay behind me and sling an arm around me. That arm and that big, solid body made me feel so safe. I closed my eyes, imagining the weight of him.

With the exception of sitting on my porch or going to the swing sets with Robin and her baby, I hadn't been out of the apartment for days. Because Robin is a germophobe, she side-eyed me when I tried to hug her last time. I should've hugged her anyway, a nice long hug to carry me over for a day or two. I remembered the good touches—my mother smoothing down my hair after carefully combing it out, the feel of a bouquet of daisies resting in my hands on my wedding day, and a memory of holding the hand of my sister Lucy as we walked through a field of grass. Lucy drowned in the shoals when I was a preschooler, so I have only that one memory of her.

I rolled over on my tummy and pushed my face into a pillow. I would have given anything to touch someone just then. George had made a habit of tracing my lower lip with his thumb, and I craved that touch. On the day George passed away, a man on his shift came to the house, his shoes still spotted with my husband's blood. Since then, I'd flashed back in my mind's eye, inserted myself into that factory, imagined holding my husband's head on my lap as he passed. *Gladly.* I'd gladly accept the touch of his blood on my fingertips.

"Hello?" Anthony said. "You still there?"

I opened my mouth to answer, but a wounded sound came out. I considered hanging up.

"Alyssa?"

"Yes."

"Everything okay?"

I nodded a moment before realizing, dumbly, that he couldn't see me. "Yeah," I told him.

"I'm so lonely during this quarantine," he said. "Have hardly been outside the past two weeks. Today, I was just staring out the window for almost an hour."

"I understand."

"You lonely? I remember you said you don't have many friends."

Had I told him that? Yes, at some point I must have. I also remembered telling him which mystery books were on my nightstand, how frustrating this furlough is, and that untrustworthiness is the worst character trait for a friend. But I also lied about things. He thinks I wear short skirts and high heels. In reality, all my clothes are modest. Nothing remotely trashy ever touches this thirty-six-year-old body of mine.

Anthony said, "You're like me. I can just tell. You're a homebody. Only sometimes you like to be out with a friend, doing quiet stuff. Walking in a park or seeing a movie."

How would this man know I enjoy parks? I vaguely remembered a conversation I'd had with him about the humongous Chattahoochee River National Forest. I'd told him that I prefer smaller parks to the large wilderness areas. It had been just a passing comment, and now I couldn't decide if I should be flattered or creeped out that he seemed to remember every little thing I mentioned to him.

"Do you know the Dekalb Farmers Market?" he asked suddenly.

"Yes," I said. "I've heard of it."

"I been there a few times and loved it. Don't know if it's open or even safe to go there right now. But when this whole mess is over, I wanna take you there. We'll spend an hour or two reading food labels, browsing produce. Then I'll bring you back here, pick you up, mmm. *God,* I want that so bad, Alyssa." Anthony gave me the minute details about what he would do to my body. Put his hand gently at my throat. Say my name. Men like him are the best lovers. No lie. You don't want a man who rushes. You want someone who will take his time, do it right. Plus, Anthony wasn't desperate for compliments like the Norwegian Minnesotan. Instead, Anthony demanded compliments. *Tell me,* he said. *Tell me now.* And then later, *Let it go. Let it all out.*

Surprisingly, by the time he cried out, I was trembling, too, my muscles down there pulsing and quaking. A wet mess.

I didn't call Anthony. It would've been unhealthy for me to hit him up, to get attached and act needy. Still, I checked my phone for the next few nights, anticipating a call from him. I could always block him later if he got too creepy. I once saw on the news where a guy was able to track his ex-girlfriend by her phone. Would Anthony be able to do that? And what about the sex? If he was one iota as good in person as he was on the phone, my eyes would roll back more than once. It had been nearly a year since George had died, and it was too hard to meet someone. Who knew when the world would be normal again? I wanted a change, some excitement, the way I used to feel so young back in my teens and twenties. Going out with friends. Laughing. Trysts in the back seats of cars.

I did end up texting him first one night. We exchanged pics, fully clothed. He had a kind smile. A sharp, pointed nose. Small, straight teeth. Slight belly.

One night, he confessed, "I'm not really eight inches."

"I figured you weren't. Guys have a tendency to embellish." I paused a moment and then asked, "Anything else I should be aware of?"

He said, "Have you always been honest with me? Is Alyssa even your real name?"

There was a long pause, and I could practically hear him rolling his eyes.

"We don't know everything about each other, and I like it that way," I said. "It's less complicated."

He began to admit other things. He hadn't had sex in a while. The last woman dumped him because she wanted exclusivity and he did not.

Days and weeks crawled by. I occasionally sat out on the porch with Robin and the baby, but Robin eventually drove them to Macon to shelter in place with her parents, leaving me all alone in the duplex for weeks. I played online Scrabble and baked and ate more desserts than should be allowed by law.

Somehow all of this has led me to the Dekalb Farmers Market on a warm day in spring of 2021. I sit in my car with the air conditioner running. Adele sings on the radio. I let my car seat back. People walk by. Families with small children. One couple holding hands and laughing.

After letting all the car windows down, I close my eyes and feel the sunshine on my cheeks and forehead. I feel a light burn on my skin.

Inside the market, colors explode. Produce bins brim in every color from dark eggplant to bright pumpkins and squashes. What a day! The scent of savory soup, maybe tomato-based, wafts out from a kitchen. I haven't eaten lunch, and the fresh-baked bread makes me lightheaded as I walk to the coffee section to meet Anthony for the first time.

I lean close to a shelf, reading the label on a package of Colombian coffee and wondering why it's so high-priced.

"Alyssa?" his voice asks from behind me.

I take a small breath and turn.

He wears a red-and-black flannel shirt, an identical pattern to the jacket George often wore. My breath catches in my throat a little, and for a second I feel like I'll scream. Every time it looks like I've turned the corner away from George's death, some little thing—a snippet of a blues song, the smell of cut grass—pops up to remind me that he's gone, and the pain clutches just as strong as it did that first day. Would it ever stop?

My hands shake a little, so I clasp them behind my back. He's staring at me with his head cocked to the side, as if he's about to ask what's wrong. I give him a half smile, but with my mask on he probably can't see it.

Anthony steps closer to me. He's wearing a surgical mask, so I can only see half of his face. I'd offer him my hand, just to feel how his would envelop it, but I don't know if it's okay to shake hands now, even though we've both been vaccinated. He wears dark denim jeans and neon-colored sneakers. As we walk the market together, I can tell he thinks I'm attractive, because his eyes run up and down my body. I decide that he's not a creeper. A creeper would stare at my breasts unabashedly, but at least this man has the decency to avert his eyes when I catch him looking.

Whenever he points out something he likes—goat cheese, enormous cucumbers, a special brand of wine—he raises his eyebrows and studies me, like he's awaiting my approval. I smile a lot, sometimes nervously.

In the parking lot, we see that we've parked on different sides. As I'm setting my Colombian coffee and package of cashews onto the seat beside me, he pulls up and asks if I want to ride to his house or follow him. "I'll follow you," I tell him.

There's so much traffic on the roads around metro Atlanta. I'm afraid I'll lose him between the stop lights. He texts his address to me just in case.

He's a careful driver, going just below the speed limit. I want to push the gas and race him down I-285. After months of being cooped up, coming out into the world again makes me feel like all those COVID days were painted gray, and today is blood orange or ruby red. My fingers tap against the steering wheel. I let my window down and smile when the air swooshes across my face and shoulders. Today my hair stands in a wild afro, so there's no need to worry about it being windblown.

On the stoop outside his large, brick house, I pause as he holds the door open for me. "My friend Robin knows where I am. She has your cell number and name. If I'm not home in a few hours, she'll have the law after you," I say, just in case.

"Sounds fair," he says, grinning.

Upstairs, we lie together, stripped down to our underwear, and watch the first of the three John Hughes movies he has. I cannot remember which film it is, but in one of them a character says, "A Black guy?" in horrified repulsion when she thinks her friend is open to dating interracially. I instantly hate her, whatever her name is. I must have a disgusted look on my face because Anthony says, "You okay?"

"This movie was better when I was a kid."

We lie together for most of that film, and he doesn't do more than kiss me, probably because he senses my nervousness. I haven't kissed anyone but George for so many years that at first it feels strange to have this new set of lips on mine. We fumble, trying to decide when to open and close our mouths. Anthony has soft lips, which soothes me. I let my shoulders down and sink farther into the mattress. He doesn't dart too much with his tongue. I like that. Without warning,

Anthony moves his lips down to my neck. *Ahh.* This man is *good.* He pulls me tighter against him. Finally, I make the move and run a hand down his body and rub him gently below the waist. He does a lot of sighing. Still no erection, though.

Quietly, he asks, “Is this just a sex thing for you, Alyssa?” He takes a deep breath. “I’m impotent. I haven’t been able to get hard since that first night we talked on the phone.”

“That *first* night? You mean you faked it the whole time, pretended to orgasm?”

He says, “I’m sorry, baby. Let me help you finish.”

I shake my head.

What had I come here for? Yes, I wanted sex. But what I really wanted was some emotionally tactile thing—the elation you get after a warm hug from someone you care about, the postcoital moment when your lover lays his head against you and you rub his head.

“Hold me,” I say.

I lie on my side, my back to him, and he puts an arm over me. Later, I hold my palm out flat to measure it against his, and I marvel that each of his fingers is an inch longer than mine. His plaid flannel shirt lies on the floor beside the bed. I resist the urge to pick it up and pull it on. As we hold hands, I close my eyes and think of the park behind my house. Though there are people in it now and have been for weeks, I pretend otherwise. Imagine otherwise. See all that wide open space. All that expanse of green with no bodies to break it up. I’m falling. Falling. Going into it. Being swallowed up.

Daughter

I'm standing in line at the pharmacy when I see a younger version of myself behind the counter. She's about twenty years old and wears a white lab coat. When she looks up, I put my face down and worry that she's looking my way. Casually, I step to the side and hide behind the man in front of me. Backing up slowly, I knock into a shelf, and bottles of vitamins rattle as they fall onto the carpet. With my back to the girl at the counter, I pick up the bottles and quietly set them back on the shelf. Never mind my Adderall prescription. I can pick it up tomorrow. Heading for the front entrance, I glance over my shoulder to see the girl counting change for a customer.

Out in my car, I take a Tylenol for what is becoming a killer tension headache. I swallow half a bottle of water and put on the air conditioning as the car idles.

I was only nineteen when I got pregnant by my boyfriend, and I didn't realize it until we'd already planned to break up. At the time, I was a college student taking a class from Dr. Dunkirk, one of those professors who communicated way too much to her students. She often invited our poetry class, all eight of us, to her home for dinner, where we sat around her big dining table and read poetry. She joked about jumping on her husband whenever she was ovulating. One time, tears welled in her eyes as we sat under the chandelier that flashed yellow light off the glasses, the silverware, and Professor Dunkirk's cheeks. She looked impossibly beautiful to me, with her upright posture. You don't often see a person so unashamed of their tears. She showed vulnerability, too, when she reached out a shaky hand to pick up her water glass. Later, Dr. Dunkirk confided to me that she and her husband had been trying for years and had miscarried twice. "I'm forty-eight," she told me. "It's probably too late for me."

A week later, I got my positive pregnancy test, and after that I offered her my child.

In the parking lot of the pharmacy, I wait in my car, hoping to get a glimpse of the girl once the employees lock up and leave for the night. I don't have to wait long. The three women all come out together, right at sunset. The girl who looks like me has taken off the lab coat and now wears a bright red sweater that is extra vibrant against her dark brown skin.

"Bye, Steph," one of the other women calls to her, and Steph waves.

My mind flashes back to the day I surrendered my daughter to Dr. Dunkirk. "We're so grateful," Dunkirk gushed. "We'll give her your name, Stephanie," she promised me. She and her husband cried over how perfect Stephanie was. And she *was* perfect. A head of thick black hair and round, pinchable cheeks, not to mention her strong arms and legs. In that moment, I wanted the child for myself. No mother can look at a baby that small without feeling protective of it and wanting to snuggle and coddle it.

Steph climbs behind the wheel of a small car parked near the pharmacy's front entrance. I hadn't planned to follow her, but in just that moment when she begins to back her car out of the spot, my curiosity gets the better of me. Where does she live? Is she still close with her parents? I couldn't imagine that she wouldn't be in close touch with them. No way would Dr. Dunkirk be anything but motherly with any child of hers. But what was Steph doing all the way out here in the country? Wouldn't she enjoy the city more? Had the Dunkirks bought a house in the country? Maybe Dr. Dunkirk had retired. It had been twenty years since I'd birthed Steph, which would put Dr. Dunkirk at sixty-eight or sixty-nine. Hard to imagine her that age.

I pull out of the parking lot behind Steph. We go through a stoplight and turn by the railroad tracks that run through town. Since they built that Walmart out by the highway, few downtown businesses have survived. We pass empty storefronts that used to house Kay's Department Store and Fenton's Hardware. Once we turn off Main Street, we're in a residential section of town. All the houses are either ranch-style or frame houses with siding. My heart beats faster. I grew up here in Muscadine in a double-wide trailer. If I'd had a better upbringing, I would have been able to keep Stephanie. I would have had the resources to give her the life I'd dreamed of as a kid. But I didn't have the money, not back then. My ex-boyfriend would not have supported me through a pregnancy, and there was no way I wanted to drop out of college and move back into that double-wide with my mama. History has a way of gluing you to a place, though. A few years after I graduated college, Mama got sick, and I moved home to care for her, reconnected with a Muscadine man, Pritchard Crawley, who would later become my husband, and settled here in town. I took comfort in the familiar faces and even took a teaching job at the old high school where I'd played basketball.

We pass the trailer park, and Steph turns onto Lee Road, a long country road that bisects a major highway. There are no cul-de-sacs and no curbs, just tall grass along the side of the roadway. She pulls into a duplex where the units look brand new. I park a few units down from her in the lot. As I open Google maps, I position my rearview mirror to get a good view of Steph. She steps out of her car, her long legs reminding me of the long-legged ex of mine who fathered her. I haven't seen him in years, hadn't bothered to tell him about the pregnancy. I was only about six or seven weeks along when he moved out, and I thought it best to not say anything. We'd been together less than a year, had an emotionally fraught relationship, and I felt glad to get rid of him.

Steph uses her key to enter the gray brick building. Who else lives here with her? Roommates? A boyfriend?

Google maps tells me I'm at 5400 Edgefield Lane. As I back up, I see the letter *F* on Steph's front door.

I save the location in my phone and head back to my house in town.

In a town this size, you can sometimes recognize the physical traits that run in people's families. Crawleys have long, narrow faces. The white set of Munsons are tanned dark with light-colored eyes, and the African American set of Munsons have light skin with plenty of moles. My daddy's family is like that to some degree, meaning that we look similar. My daddy was a Craig, and sometimes when I go to the grocery or the Walmart, strangers ask if I'm kin to any Craigs. We each have an oval-shaped face with a high forehead and deep-set black eyes beneath straight, black eyebrows. When I saw those intense Craig eyes on Stephanie at the drugstore, I hid from her for fear that she'd recognize that we look so much alike. In hindsight, I suppose hiding from Stephanie sounds like a nutty thing to do. She hasn't seen me since she was an infant, and unless her parents told her my name, I don't see how she would know who I am.

Several times during Steph's infancy, Dr. Dunkirk invited me over to see her, but I always made some excuse or didn't answer her calls. Pretty soon, she got the message and stopped trying. Dr. Dunkirk probably thought I was ashamed of my decision or that thinking of Stephanie caused me too much pain. No, it's not that I'm *ashamed* of giving Steph up. I'm proud. My ex-boyfriend would've asked me to get an abortion; I'm certain he would've. I didn't want to abort the baby, and I couldn't keep Steph either. I made the *right* choice. So why did I reject Dr. Dunkirk's offer to let me know my daughter? It's because of my upbringing. I always felt the need to keep what I did secret from my family. My parents, both long-dead now, would not have approved. My mother would've judged me especially harshly for giving up my baby. I didn't want her quoting scripture to me or asking me to move in with her and raise the child, so I stayed in Atlanta and away from my family during the pregnancy. Also, though I would not have admitted it back then, I was afraid of what Steph would think of me as she got older. I feared her resentment. When measured against the Dunkirks, with their summer trips and private school educations, I'd never be seen as successful or even competent. I was a failure.

After I see Stephanie at the pharmacy that first time, I keep inventing reasons to go back there. I sit on a bench by the blood-pressure cuff near the magazine racks and watch her. She's not a pharmacist. She never gives consultations to the customers, and whenever she has a question she'll ask another worker for help. Stephanie is probably a cashier or a pharmacy tech.

I wear my darkest sunglasses inside the pharmacy, which is probably silly. I try to summon the courage to pick up my prescription, but I keep chickening out. My text alert says it was filled several days ago, and I hope they haven't restocked it yet. The Adderall helps me focus. I wasn't diagnosed with Asperger's until I was in graduate school, and I can definitely do without the medicine, but it sure makes life easier.

Thank God, Stephanie did not inherit my social awkwardness. Often, she smiles at the pharmacy customers while making eye contact and chitchatting. Once, she spends several minutes searching for an internet coupon to help an older woman save ten dollars on vitamins. I'm not at all surprised to see that Steph is a sweet girl, a good person. Of course she is. She was raised by the venerable Dr. Dunkirk.

One day, I take a deep breath and step up to the counter. The girl in the white lab coat isn't Steph. She has red hair and wears a nametag that says "Grace," and I feel relieved that Steph's car wasn't in the lot and she doesn't appear to be working that day. I pull off my sunglasses and put them on the counter as I open my wallet.

"I'm Stephanie Craig," I begin. "I'm here to pick up my—"

The girl named Grace cuts me off by leaning back to speak to someone who is out of my line of sight. "Steph," she calls through a doorway. "Your mom's here."

My heart leaps up into my throat. I shake my head so hard my hoop earrings beat against my cheeks.

"What?" asks Stephanie as she comes into my view. She looks at me, and I drop my eyes to the counter. "Where?" Steph says in a high-pitched voice similar to the voice I had as a girl.

"Oh," Grace says and giggles. She puts my prescription down on the counter in front of me. "She has your name," the girl says. "And I just assumed she was your mama since y'all look alike."

I slowly lift my eyes to meet Stephanie's. She gives me a once over. "That's not my mama," she says, and I admire the southern way she pronounces the word *mama.*

"Pay her no attention, ma'am," Stephanie says, grinning at me. "She thinks all Black folks look alike." She cuts up laughing, and Grace rings up my prescription for me. I pay and then grin at them as I turn to leave. "She even has your dimple," Grace says, her voice fading as I step out of earshot.

That night, I look up Dr. Dunkirk on Facebook and consider messaging her. Her page says she is indeed retired. There are older pictures of her vacationing with her husband, Gerard, and both are smiling on beaches and standing in front of landmarks like the Gateway Arch and Big Ben and the Space Needle. I scroll down and see that Gerard passed away about two years ago. Someone posted the funeral announcement and there are dozens of comments from people offering condolences and talking about what a good man he was.

In the early days of social media, I considered looking for Steph and Dr. Dunkirk, but I always found an excuse not to. I was convinced I'd find pictures of Stephanie hugging her parents and smiling. It's silly to have felt such jealousy, but I felt it. Though my child has always been in my heart and I knew she was probably living her best life, I also knew I wasn't strong enough to see the evidence of that best life. Seeing her with her parents would painfully remind me that she wasn't *with me.* I felt robbed, even though I was the one who'd surrendered my most valued possession. Seeing Steph at the pharmacy forced me to confront all those feelings and curiosities I've had over the years. I tell myself I'm mature enough to look at her Facebook page now. I take a deep breath, search her name, and find her account. I click on Steph's page, but most of her info is private. The public info shows me the political memes and cat videos she's posted. I already know a good deal about her—first and last name, address, and even her birthday. She was born two days after my twentieth birthday, which means she'll be turning twenty-one soon. Our birthdays are coming up next month, and I imagine sending her a gift. Maybe I could put it in her mailbox or just buy something on Amazon and have it shipped to her. I never had any other children, though I always wanted a daughter, someone to shop with and share secrets with. For a moment, I'm swept up in a fantasy in which I buy the two of us a spa day at a winery outside town. "Thanks, Mama," she'll say, beaming at me. The smile is, of course, followed by a long hug.

Halfway through composing an instant message to Stephanie, I stop and put my head in my hands. How do I even know she would respond to me after all these years? I was the one who stopped taking Dr. Dunkirk's phone calls. It's probably too late to be in her life now.

I erase the draft of the instant message and power off the laptop.

One day I'm sitting on the bench at the pharmacy, pretending to read a copy of the *Muscadine Weekly Herald* when I overhear Steph telling Grace about an exercise class she's taking. "It's like Zumba," Steph says. "But it's not just Latin music. We dance to a lot of hip-hop, too." "Pleeease come dance with me, Gracie," she whines. "It'll be fun."

Grace shakes her head and laments being a poor dancer. Steph counters that by giving her the days and the time of the dance classes she takes at the county rec center.

"Mondays, Wednesdays, and Fridays at five," I repeat to myself.

The county rec center isn't a place I frequent. I'm a smoker who doesn't exercise if I can help it, but on Friday I show up wearing cotton shorts, a T-shirt, and sneakers. I'd planned to work out, but I'm late due to the twenty minutes I spent nearly talking myself out of it. I recognize Steph's red Ford Fusion, and I deliberately park several rows behind her car. The website had said the classes would be in room B, and when I enter the red brick building I ask the girl at the desk to point it out to me.

"I just want to observe for today, if that's possible," I say.

She nods and points to my left. "It's the last door at the end of the hall," she explains.

I walk down the corridor toward a room with techno dance music thumping from it. The drumbeats are bouncing off the walls. The room has several large plate-glass windows, and the door stands open. A group of older women smile through the open doorway at something. When I get closer, I see that the women are admiring a group of people in the dance class. Steph is among the dancers, and she wears an oversized red T-shirt and tight spandex shorts. She moves forward deliberately, her hips in sync with the loud beat of drums. There are several other women in the class, but I can't take my eyes off her. She's that good. A sheen of sweat has gathered on her dark skin, which makes it appear to glow. The music increases in intensity, and Steph moves her feet faster, matching the bass rhythm. Suddenly, she jumps, lands with her ankles crossed, and spins around. I draw in my breath along with the other women watching, and we exchange smiles. "That's my daughter," I whisper to myself, but as soon as I say it, I realize it's a mistake. The older white lady with the gray, poufy hair points at Steph, who is the only Black girl in the group.

"She's beautiful," the lady says to me.

"Thanks," I mumble.

I watch until the class ends. The dancers finish their stretches, and as I'm turning to go, the lady says, "Are you joining this class with your daughter?"

I turn to look at her, and she's standing right beside Steph, who has now come out into the hallway. Steph stares at me and again I'm struck by how much we look alike. Very strong African features. Years ago, I had a Somali friend in college who asked if I was Somali, too. If you've ever seen stereotypically Somali features, then you know what

I mean. Smooth, dark skin that looks as though it has no pores. Silky black curls. Steph and I aren't Somali, not that I know of, but our features are similar to that.

Studying my daughter's face, I open my mouth to answer the woman, but then I think better of it and flee.

"Hey!" someone yells from behind me, and that one syllable is enough to let me know it's her voice. Stephanie's.

I pretend to not hear her as I push through the exit door at the end of the corridor.

The hot air hits my face and arms as soon as I leave the climate-controlled building.

"Hey," the voice says again.

Instincts tell me to keep going, but I stop running, swallow hard, and turn to face her.

Her eyes aren't giving me the once-over the way they did that day at the pharmacy. Right now, she's scrutinizing me, all the way down to my legs, which are heavier than hers and not nearly as toned. She says, "I know who you are."

I nod stupidly, wetting my dry lips with my tongue before croaking out, "I just wanted to see what your life is like."

The woman with the poufy hair stands beside a nearby car, hearing every word.

"Do you drink coffee?" I ask. "There's a coffee shop," I trail off, pointing in the general direction of the one downtown.

"Jerry's?" she asks.

"Y-yeah. I went to high school with him. I've known his family for years. My daddy used to fish with his granddaddy back when Three Forks was just," I pause because I've said all this without taking a breath and because I should probably wait for her to offer some sign that she even remotely cares.

Steph's eyebrow is raised and she stares at me. "I don't drink coffee much," she says.

"Oh," I say.

The spying lady opens her car door and eases it closed once she's climbed into the car. She just sits there with her window down.

"Do you have pictures of him?" Steph asks. "Pictures of my daddy?"

I nod slowly. "I don't have any with me, but I could bring you some sometime."

She turns as if she's leaving but then turns back to me. "You could buy me an ice cream," she says.

So we take our cars down to the Dairy Queen, where she orders a chocolate-dipped cone and we sit in a booth. Families with children crowd the restaurant. My tennis shoe keeps sticking to a spill beneath our table. One little boy drops a French fry on the floor and pops it in his mouth before his mother can stop him. The drive-thru window is only a couple of paces behind us, and a huge pickup truck idles in the window, its obnoxious engine causing me to lean forward to hear Stephanie.

She licks her cone while keeping her eyes on me and says, "I scrapbook. I have a dozen books of pictures already. I take them on my phone and print them at work," she explains.

The conversation seems so trivial. I'd been preparing myself to answer questions about why I gave her up, questions about her father, and had even prepared myself for some level of resentment hurled at me. If there is any rabid curiosity or resentment in her, I see no signs of it.

"Should I bring the pictures to the pharmacy?" I ask her. "I have a photo album of my family pictures, but only a few of your dad," I say, pausing awkwardly. It feels strange to call my ex-boyfriend her dad, even though that's what he is. "I could bring them to the pharmacy tomorrow, if you'd want that."

She nods.

We arrange to meet during her lunchtime at Jefferson's, a downtown restaurant. I get there early, and when she arrives I rise and try to go in for a hug, but she sticks out her hand instead.

I treat her to a sandwich, soup, and a Coke. She brings two scrapbooks. One has a sorority theme, and there are dozens of photos of her and her AKA sorority sisters. There are program announcements for dances and fundraisers, and ticket stubs for Lizzo and Dua Lipa concerts. I'm surprised to see she goes to Paulson College, the same historically Black college I attended.

"That's a long commute for you, isn't it?" I ask.

She shrugs. "It's only an hour and a half." She clears her throat. "Mama got sick last year, so I moved out here to the country to take care of her."

"You live with your mama?" I ask, trying to imagine Dr. Dunkirk in the little duplex where Steph lives.

"Yeah," she says. "After my daddy passed, she wanted to get out of the city. I guess our old house made her sad," she explained.

I nod, flipping through her scrapbook. The girls look so young, even younger than sorority girls did when I was that age. "This one is my favorite," I tell her, pointing to a picture of her in a sash and heavy makeup. She wears a crown on her head. The deep dimple in her cheek and the way she cocks her head to the side remind me of myself at that age.

She excuses herself to go to the restroom, and I unstick the pageant picture and put it in my purse. When she comes back to the table, I'm flipping through the other album. The theme for this one is a cruise she took with her mama and another elderly lady. Seeing her together with Dr. Dunkirk makes my heart ache. I can't name this feeling as anything but jealousy.

Steph's questions flow freely for the rest of her lunch hour. She already knows her father's name, but she wants to know where he lives now and what work he does. I can't answer those questions because I haven't kept in touch with him. She's tried to find him on Facebook over the years, but the name Mike Thomas is so common that it's nearly impossible. She tells me she's tried to look me up, but couldn't find me either. I confess that I didn't get Facebook until very recently. She pauses briefly to look at the two pictures I have of her daddy and then flips casually through my family photo book. To my dismay, she doesn't appear too interested in pictures of me. Instead, she pauses to stare at some of the older pictures. Her eyes linger for a long while on a black-and-white photo of my grandmother taken in a cotton field. Though it's one of only a few pictures I have of Grandma, I pull it from its sleeve and give it to Stephanie, along with the two photos of her father.

She looks worried about something, and when I ask what's wrong, things start to spill out of her. Her mother's dying of cancer and medical bills have eaten away all of their money. She may quit school because they can't pay tuition.

"Oh no," I say, reaching across the table to pat her hand. She doesn't pull away, so I just sit there squeezing her hand every now and again.

"Can I do something to help you?" I ask.

She studies my face a moment, as if deciding how much I really mean it. "Well," she hesitates. "I'm able to pay the rent on my duplex with my pharmacy check, but I can't pay my tuition, and I don't want to quit school."

"How much do you need?" I ask, surprising even myself with how willing I am to give her the money. I'm by no means wealthy, but my ex-husband, Pritchard, did leave me some money, and I've never been a big spender. After fifteen years of teaching, I do have quite a bit in my accounts.

She shakes her head. "I couldn't ask for your help." For the first time, she squeezes my hand.

"I want to," I say. "I want to help put you through school."

She hesitates again. "Tuition is pretty expensive," she says.

I nod. "Why don't I give you the money for next semester?"

She pauses to consider it.

I *owe* her this. I'm her mother, after all, and shouldn't I be there to help when she needs it?

"Okay," she whispers finally.

She pushes some buttons on her phone and calls out the balance of her tuition and fees. It's a little over $8,000.

I write her the check.

Before she leaves to go back to work, I get her phone number so that we can keep in touch. Halfway to the front of the restaurant, she comes back to hug me, and I wish I could hold on to her longer, but she pulls away after a few seconds.

I text her a few times over the weekend. She always answers back, though not always right away. I ask her about taking the spa day with me, and she replies enthusiastically that she'd love to.

On Monday night, I type a Facebook message to Dr. Dunkirk. My perspective has changed now that I know she's sick. I'll apologize for not being there for Steph, but I'll assure her that I'm here for her now. I type:

"Hi, it's Stephanie Craig, Steph's birth mother. I ran into her here in town, and she mentioned that you're sick. If there's anything I can do to help you, let me know."

As I'm waiting for her response, I send a Facebook friend invite to Steph.

A few minutes later, as I'm scrolling through Dr. Dunkirk's page, I get the message notification from her. I open the tab, and the message reads:

"It's good to hear from you, Stephanie. I've often thought of you over the years. Sadly, I haven't had contact with my daughter for a while. What's your phone number? Can I call you right now?"

I give her my number and wait for my cell to ring. Steph said her mother lived with her, and Dr. Dunkirk was now telling me that they hadn't seen each other for a while. How long is a while? Days? Weeks?

My phone rings and I snatch it up to answer it.

"Hey, Stephanie?" says a woman's voice, and I recognize it as Dr. Dunkirk's. Funny how I can recall her voice after all these years. She liked to begin our classes by reading a poem aloud, and I can still remember her inflections on some of the words.

I jump right in, telling her what Steph revealed to me at the diner the other day. "I was so sorry to hear about your illness," I say. "How are you feeling? Stephanie told me you've been sick. With cancer. Is it in remission now?"

She doesn't answer right away, and for a second I wonder if the call has dropped.

Dr. Dunkirk sighs and then launches into it: "Stephanie is a very inventive liar. You can't believe anything she says."

Anything?

"I wish I could tell you that she turned into a lovely person, but she—" she pauses and lets out her breath. "She lies. She won't study. She left school. I can't do anything to coax her back, and—"

"She told me y'all didn't have the money for tuition."

She gives me the frustrated sigh again and says, "When her father passed away, he left a college fund for her, but I won't give her the money if she's not enrolled in school."

For the next half hour we talk about everything Steph told me at the restaurant, and her mother denies most of it. No, Dr. Dunkirk has never had cancer. No, she doesn't live with Steph. Dunkirk still lives in the same old house in metro Atlanta where we sat under her kitchen chandelier. Mother and daughter have not seen each other in nearly a year. Steph left school when she left her mama's house last year. I don't tell her about the $8,000 I gave Stephanie. We say goodbye and hang up.

My eyes well with tears. It hurts that Stephanie would lie to me so easily. How *stupid* am I to have fallen for it?

I open online banking on my phone and see that the check has already cleared. The little scammer either cashed it or deposited it this morning. My pulse thumps against my temple, and I take several deep breaths to calm down.

I go to my purse and take out the photo of Steph wearing the tiara. She looks so happy and carefree. At my dresser, I slide the photo into the corner of the mirror.

She's a young girl with a dead father and she's estranged from her mother. "She needs that money more than I do," I whisper to my quiet bedroom.

I sit up a lot of nights, staring at my phone, hoping that Steph will reach out to me. She doesn't. When I message her, I get only her silence in return.

School starts back again, and I throw myself into work—volunteer to sit on various committees, volunteer for two afterschool programs.

I don't see Steph at the pharmacy anymore, and I ask Grace about her. Grace confirms that she's quit but doesn't know where she works now.

Some nights, when I feel especially lonely, I get in my car and drive the country roads, windows down, sipping hot coffee. Usually, I find my way to Steph's duplex, where I sit in my car and watch the yellow light burning through her front curtain. I consider knocking on her front door, but what could I say to bring her back to me? One night I see the outline of her in the front window. I know her by the curls that frame her head. I know her by the long, lean body. Does she see my car? Would she recognize it if she did?

She has company some nights. Sometimes the visitor is a young man who greets her with hugs and kisses, and his car is still there when I depart late at night. Other times, the visitor is a young woman who bounces into the apartment when Steph opens the door.

I buy Stephanie the spa day. She can get a manicure and pedicure and a facial. She can even get an hour-long massage and lounge in the sauna. I have the gift certificate shipped to her address, and I put my return address on it, just in case she wants to contact me. I fantasize about a Cape Cod–style home with a wide front porch, perfect for sitting out there with my daughter. She could stop over any evening that she wants, and I will buy us a couple of rocking chairs. Rocking together, we'll watch the sun go down as the sky turns pink over the Blue Ridge Mountains. I fantasize about getting Mother's Day cards and Christmas cards from Stephanie. Maybe one day she'll send me a scrapbook with big, red hearts drawn on it. It will be pink with silver glitter that rubs off on my hands.

Gullah Babies

Granny and I were on our front porch shucking corn one day when I said, "Granny, there's a new boy at my school. His name's Mark." I smiled down at my lap, twisted a few strands of the corn silks around my pointer finger. "We're friends."

"He white or colored?" she asked.

Granny was in her seventies by that time, and she and the old folks on the island were the only ones I'd heard who used the word *colored. White or colored? Colored or white?* The only thing that ever bothered me about Granny was that she was so hung up on race.

"He's Black," I answered her.

I thought I saw a small glimmer of relief flash across Granny's face as she reached up to adjust the red, orange, and yellow scarf tied around her head.

"He in the grade with you or older?"

"Same age as me. He's in my class." I sighed, tried to decide if just then was a good time to ask what I needed to ask.

"I was wondering, can Mark come over this weekend? He wants to see where I live."

She ripped away a corn husk and paused to look at me. With her dark brown fingers wrapped around the yellow corn, and the silks strewn over her wrist, Granny made a pretty picture.

"I reckon so," she said. "Are you gon' bring him to worship with us?"

Mark had said his parents were Catholics, and strict about it, too. Would they allow Mark to come to our church?

"I'll ask him," I said.

On Sunday, the day that Mark was supposed to come in on the ferry, rain was forecasted. None of the houses on the island had paved yards or driveways, just loosely scattered gravel, sandy dirt, and grass. I was used to a mushy yard whenever it rained, but Mark was a town boy. I would be embarrassed for him to get his feet all muddy in my yard.

I held my breath before I pulled my bedroom curtain back. But no such luck. Water had pooled up around the porch. Granny's Easter lilies were drowned. Rain ran off the eaves of my cousin Victoria's house and into a big puddle in her side yard. Vic's dog Mitzie, a black lab, lay on their back porch. When Mitzie noticed me watching her from the window, she lifted her head and thumped her tail against the slatted floor of the porch.

I took a yellow sundress from my closet, one that Vic had given me last summer for my sixteenth birthday. Vic had sewn the dress from lightweight cotton fabric with light brown pinstripes running through it. The dress was the prettiest thing I owned, and I'd been saving it to wear for a special occasion.

I took the dress into the bathroom, showered, and stepped into it. I walked into the kitchen to ask Granny's help with the zipper. Bacon sizzled on the stove, and flour dusted the counter. The back screen door whined open and bumped closed. A second later, Vic came into the kitchen wearing a red raincoat. Vic and I were seventeen and only two months apart in age.

"Hey, y'all," Vic said as Granny zipped my dress. She gave Granny a kiss on the cheek.

Vic waited until after Granny had stepped into the bedroom and then whispered to me, "Will he sleep in your bedroom tonight?"

"*What?*"

"Mark. Is he staying overnight?" Vic asked.

I almost swallowed my tongue at the idea of Mark sleeping with me. I said, "Why don't you ask Granny?"

"Hell no," Vic said. "She'd bust my ass with a whisk broom." Vic fingered her stubby black braid. Her lilac-colored nails shone under the overhead light.

I sat down with her at the kitchen table. As I buttered a biscuit, someone tapped on the back door.

"Come in!" we both yelled.

Before the door opened I knew it was Jeremy Boudreaux, or J.J., as we called him. He'd promised to drive Vic and me over to the ferry. A tall, thin boy, J.J. was a year older than we were, and he'd just graduated high school the month before. He'd be shipping off to basic training for the army the next day. His leaving had been all anyone on our island had talked about for weeks. We all loved J.J. It was impossible not to. Quiet and thoughtful, he never said a bad word about anyone.

J.J. came over to the table and looked down at me. I got a clear view of the scar underneath his chin, the one he'd gotten from falling off his bike when we were little. J.J. was lighter skinned than me, and his eyes were a lighter shade of brown.

He grabbed the bun at the nape of my neck and tugged on it. "Hey, Snaggle," he said.

I rolled my eyes at the old nickname. Once when I was six, I'd lost a tooth during a church dinner. Not knowing what to do with it, I'd leaned over and dropped it on J.J.'s dinner plate.

J.J. broke a biscuit in half. A layer of steam rose above his thumbs. He ate the biscuit in three big bites. I ate my bacon biscuit and stared out the kitchen window at the rain.

"C'mon, y'all. Ferry'll be coming in soon," J.J. said.

I grabbed my umbrella and my leather sandals. I put them in my oversized purse, slipped on a pair of rain boots, and followed Vic and J.J. outside.

At least Vic had the good sense to wear a rain jacket with a hood. I cursed myself for running out of the house without mine. My umbrella bent in on itself, and I got soaked. The rain poured so heavily I could hardly see. We piled into the truck's cab and just sat there, waiting for the rain to slow down. Water dripped into my eyes and rolled down my face and neck. Vic rooted around in the glove compartment and found some napkins for us to dry off with.

I'd wear my boots until we got to the ferry station, then I'd pull on the sandals and leave the mud-caked boots in Jeremy's truck. Back in fifth grade, on the very first day I'd boarded the mainland school bus, a white girl had looked at me and asked, "What's wrong with your shoes?"

Shamed by her question, I looked down at my worn, unraveling shoelaces and at the little clumps of wet sand on my sneakers. I'd left a sandy path down the center aisle to my bus seat. Embarrassment caused tears to well behind my eyes. As I grew older, I became more conscious of how I looked to others. I couldn't run around wild-haired and barefooted off island the way I could at home. No more braless days or wrinkled shorts or dirty shoes for me.

Finally, the rain subsided and J.J. inched us along toward the ferry dock. The main road leading toward the ferry was paved, but the driveways and side roads were all sand. The wipers made a comforting sound as a few drops of water splashed on the windshield.

When I was growing up on Pittman's Pointe, the only people I ever saw around the island were my own aunts, uncles, and cousins. And, of course, the "vacation people." The vacationers rented one of my cousin Florie's two camper trailers. They came to fish, ride on the bike trail over behind Florie's house, or just to have a secluded place to relax. Our island was one of the few along the coast that wasn't a commercial tourist resort, and we planned to keep it that way. My family owned about two-thirds of the land, and we prided ourselves on never selling. From the time I was little bitty, Granny and the old folks always said we didn't want to become another Tybee Island or a St. Simon's, that we didn't want too many summer people coming in with noise and traffic.

When we got to the ferry, I didn't realize I'd forgotten to change my shoes until Mark stepped onto the platform and looked down at my muddy boots. His eyes traveled up to my face, and he smiled. Rain drizzled down on us; he wiped it from his brow.

Mark was very dark, like me. He had broad cheekbones and a strong chin.

"Did you have a nice ride over?" I asked him, after we'd said our hellos and began to walk to the truck.

Mark looked around at the water and sand as though he were in a completely new world.

"Ferry ride took about fifteen minutes, just like you said. It's pretty here, so close to the water. How big is the island?"

The rain had cleared for a moment, and we all paused when we got to the truck.

"It's about four miles long and three miles wide," I told him. "J.J. can ride us around a little after church."

"Let me guess," he said, smirking. "There's only one church, right?"

I nodded. "Fifty-four people live on the island."

"Fifty people!" Mark said. "Wow. You really do live in a nowhere swamp."

"It ain't a swamp," J.J. said. "It's an island mostly full of woods and marshes."

If Mark noticed J.J.'s annoyed tone, he didn't show it. Instead, Mark asked, "Are you guys really inbred? At school they say everyone here is your cousin."

Something rolled over in my belly. I looked at J.J. and then at Vic. Both waited, silently, to see how I'd respond.

"My momma's people are Pittmans," I explained to Mark. "But I'm related to everyone here in some way or other. I won't marry someone from the island, though." I said this last sentence with an eyeroll: "I'm not inbred; none of us are."

When I was four, Mama ran off to live with Daddy in Muscadine, Georgia, which was Daddy's hometown. I always hated explaining my family situation to people because they usually looked at me with pity.

We drove the main road home, straight across the middle of the island. Forest lined the highway for almost two miles, and then it gave way to open expanses of sand once we got closer to home.

"On the way to the ferry dock, we drove past the old slave block on the mainland. Did your family come in through there?" Mark asked me.

"Probably so," I told him.

"You ever want to research and find out? I mean, if I thought my folks were bought and sold here, I'd want to know."

I loved history as much as the next person, but I didn't want to research every little detail about my ancestors' suffering. Thelma Pittman, my great-grandmama, knew everything about the island. She could've told Mark anything he wanted to know. But I never took the opportunity to research anything. All I had were family stories. That was enough.

J.J. answered for me: "I would *never* want to know where my folks were bought and sold." He looked pointedly at Mark.

Mark's brow furrowed with what I thought at first was anger but then realized was just thoughtfulness.

I couldn't help but think that Mark had only come to the island to gawk at us. How had I not noticed what he was in school? Probably because I'd only known him two weeks. How silly of me to think I had any idea of what sort of boy he was. Still, I tried to give him the benefit of the doubt. Maybe our lives were so foreign to him that he couldn't help but ask a passel of silly questions.

The smell of coffee greeted me as soon as we walked in the kitchen door. Granny put out her hand for Mark to shake. She said, "You the one from up north?"

Mark leaned toward her, a confused look on his face, and then looked at me. Granny repeated herself, and when he still didn't understand, Vic repeated Granny's words to him.

Everyone from our part of Georgia understood Gullah accents, so no one we knew had trouble with Granny's speech. Mark's ignorance made me defensive. Was he judging her?

As Mark ate the breakfast Granny had made, Granny stared at him, eyes squinted, biting her lower lip. Suspicious of outsiders to the point of paranoia, she always seemed annoyed with their questions.

After he'd eaten a second buttered biscuit, Mark laid his shoulders back against his chair and said, "Delicious."

Granny grinned. She was the best cook on the island and knew it. When summer people came, everyone in the neighborhood recommended her special plate—peanut stew and yellow rice with red peas.

Mark asked, "Do you have police on the island?"

When I shook my head no, he asked, "So what would happen if there was a robbery or something?"

"You planning on robbing somebody while you're here?" J.J. asked.

Mark grinned and said, "No, just curious."

Granny said, "We don't have much crime here. That Shackleford boy what lives over by the marsh took a grill off somebody's back porch one time, but his mama beat him so hard he carried it back."

Mark didn't say anything, and I wondered if he understood Granny.

J.J. said, "This is a good place. I haven't heard about any crime since my family moved here."

"You're not from here?" Mark asked.

"My daddy was old army buddies with a guy from here. When the guy died, he left the general store on the island to my daddy. We moved here to run the store when I was five."

"Was it the store by the road we drove in on? The little blue building?"

"Yep, only store on the island."

As we ate, J.J. kept giving Mark the same squinty-eyed look that Granny had given him, that look of suspicion and distrust.

During church that morning, Mark looked confused any time an older person spoke to him. Being from Boston, Mark occasionally had trouble with the southern accents at our school, but Gullah seemed to puzzle him even more than a typical Georgia accent.

We began devotional service with a spiritual hymn called "On My Journey Home." Usually, Deacon Sylvester Mason or his brother Charlie Mason led the song by singing a line or two. Then, we all joined in to repeat the words sung by the deacon. After we sang a few verses, we moaned our way through the rest of the song. The words were gibberish, but the intonations were pretty and soulful. I never thought of the song or the way we sang it as being odd or funny, but Mark got the giggles.

"This is the silliest song I ever heard," he whispered to me. "Sounds like those songs in old movies. I feel like we should all be out picking cotton."

Mark started moaning louder. When I raised my voice to meet his, he gave me a wink. And because that wink was everything, I moaned even louder.

Mark leaned toward me, close enough to kiss and said, "I'm having fun."

Miss Eugenia, in the pew in front of us, stood and swayed from side to side, one hand raised toward the ceiling. Granny had told me that people waved their hands that way when they felt the spirit of God. The only strong feeling I'd ever had in church was a headache, especially when people shouted at the end of preaching.

Mark continued to moan loudly, and Miss Eugenia turned and looked at us. Her straw hat was angled slantwise over her forehead, a look that I thought always gave her face a soft, elegant shape. She narrowed her eyes for a second, no doubt wondering why he was so loud.

I smiled at her. She returned the smile and faced forward again.

During preaching, Mark kept poking me and leaning over to whisper to me. At one point, he described how he'd skinned his leg playing baseball the day before. "See," he said in a loud whisper, rolling up his pant leg to reveal a jagged scratch the length of my pinky. He pantomimed sliding into base. He stuck his arms out in front of us and bugged his eyes out. I laughed loudly, even though it wasn't all that funny.

Vic, who sat on my other side, patted me lightly on the forearm. "Y'all hush," she whispered.

But it was too late.

From behind the pulpit, Reverend Means said, "I wish y'all would be quiet back there, young people."

Half the congregation turned to look at Mark and me.

I looked at Granny, who sat in her usual space near the pulpit. Because I never got into much trouble, Granny rarely punished me. Whenever I did some little thing she disapproved of—scored less than an A on a test or skipped church—she let me know it by her expression. Just then, she squeezed her lips together. A muscle twitched in her jaw.

After the preaching, I told Granny that Vic, J.J., and I were taking Mark down to the beach. She nodded but wouldn't look at me. I knew she'd wait until Mark was long gone on the ferry that afternoon before giving me a talking to. Granny wasn't the sort to berate me in front of everyone.

There were two wide beaches on the island, and we chose the one on north island because of its proximity to the church. The boys went down to the surf. Vic and I sat on the little plank porch, the one Granny always said my great-granddaddy had built. I felt proud whenever I sat on it. Though I'd never known Great-Granddaddy Pittman, sitting at this place he'd made with his own hands made me feel close to him. I wondered if he was a romantic like me, someone who liked to lie back and look out at the water and think about love and the future.

"Can't believe you and Mark were so loud during meeting," Vic said.

"He was telling me about a baseball game."

"I heard. Whole church did." She looked out at Mark. He and J.J. had rolled up their pant legs and were standing ankle-deep in the surf. "He's judging us," she said. "He's been judging us all day. And for that I don't like him, but he's your friend, your soon-to-be boyfriend, so the only person who has to like him is you." Then she said, "J.J.'s jealous. He's been giving Mark the stank eye."

Ever since the year I had turned twelve and got boobs, Vic said J.J. liked me as more than friends. She claimed his shyness silenced him.

Mark took off his shirt and jogged up to the porch to lay it on the bench, the only dry place around. "Hey, Lena," he said. "Ever skinny-dip?"

I looked at Vic, who bit back a smile.

I shook my head no.

"You scared?" Mark asked.

"No."

"Then why not?" he asked.

J.J. walked closer to hear what we were talking about.

"Says she won't skinny-dip," Mark told J.J.

"Smart girl," J.J. said.

Mark pulled off his shorts and flung them onto the porch rail. He took off running toward the water, then trudged through it, ankle-deep, wearing only his boxers.

The three of us threw back our heads and laughed.

"Cute butt!" I called after him.

"What butt?" Vic asked. "He's got nothing back there."

Once he was waist-high in the water, Mark turned back and shouted, "C'mon in." He looked straight at me when he said it. For a moment, there was only the two of us. His smile. His confidence. My heart, thumping so hard I felt it in my ribcage.

Everything about Mark made me want to be defiant and carefree, the same as he was. I stood and reached back to unzip my dress.

"What are you doing?" J.J. asked.

"Oh, come on. It'll be fun. Don't you want to try something different?"

I got the dress halfway unzipped, then leaned back toward Vic for her help.

"Why are you doing this?" she asked, her hands in her lap.

"You two can be sticks in the mud. I want to have fun."

Becoming more frustrated with the dress, I pulled my arms out of it, then twisted it around so the zipper faced me. I stepped out of the dress and left it there on the porch. I didn't dare take off my bra and underwear. I wasn't that bold, or that crazy.

Out in the water, Mark grabbed my head and dunked me under, which pissed me off because I didn't want my hair wet.

"Let's race to that little strip of land," he said, pointing to an isle about a hundred yards out.

It was a tiny, grassy strip. I'd never swum that far. No one I knew had ever dared.

"Scared?" he asked.

When I hesitated, he said, "We could race."

Without waiting for my answer, he drew in a big breath and dove under.

I looked back at Vic and J.J. One of them had picked up my dress and hung it neatly on the porch rail. The dress and Mark's pants whipped back and forth in the breeze.

After several seconds, Mark still had not surfaced. I was just about to go under and hunt for him when he came up a few feet to my right.

"I think we better head back. Looks like rain," I said, pointing up at the clouds.

"Nah, a little rain won't hurt us," he said. "Come race me. Please, baby?"

He'd never called me baby before.

I wondered how long it would take me to swim out to the isle. I was a strong swimmer, had been since I was a little girl. And wasn't Mark my guest? I wanted him to have fun. So far, all we'd done was eat breakfast and go to Sunday meeting. He'd never want to come back here. He'd never want to spend time with boring old me ever again.

"I'll do it," I said.

He smiled big at me. "Ready?"

I made sure my arms were level with his. He kept inching his body forward, and I did the same.

"Get set," he said.

A raindrop hit my forehead and ran down my nose. Little drops sprinkled my arms and shoulders.

"Go!" he yelled, taking off, splashing water back into my face.

He had a head start, but once I'd swum half a dozen breast strokes I came level with him.

I focused on breathing. Breathing and thrusting. Kicking.

From the corner of my eye, his dark shape began to slow, or maybe I was moving better once I'd gotten warmed up. I closed my eyes. Pretty soon I developed a rhythm.

Breathe. Thrust. Kick.

Breathe. Thrust. Kick.

When my eyes opened again, I was pretty close to the isle, but when I looked to my right, I didn't see him anywhere. Still moving forward, I turned my head left.

No Mark. No sign of him.

I stopped swimming and looked back. It was a wonder how far I'd come. The sky had gone completely gray. Rain came down steadily. Though it was still early afternoon, the overcast sky had created a twilight.

Then, I saw Mark pull himself from the water and walk up the beach. He must've been over a hundred yards away. Through the rain and gray twilight, the distance seemed somehow farther than it had originally been. I became aware of what a stupid thing I'd done, like that time I climbed a tree, kept climbing higher and higher to see how far I could go. Finally, when I looked down, I was stunned by the space between my body and the ground. The tops of the houses were all patched, and I could see clear to the ferry dock and the church.

When they saw me stop in the water, Vic and J.J. waved. How far away they were. Their tiny shapes sat on the porch, shielded from the rain. I couldn't tell if they were cheering me on or asking, "What the hell?!" Probably the latter.

Mark had given up. But I wouldn't. I'd prove I could do something he didn't have the guts to do.

I started swimming toward the little isle again. This time much slower, knowing that it wasn't a race anymore. It was about endurance and courage, not speed. I stopped several times and looked, in awe, to my left and right. Nothing but water as far as my eyes could see. The water and sky were both gray, and looking out on the horizon I could barely distinguish the line that separated the gray water from the gray sky. In the spaces all around me, rain pebbled the ocean, coming down and then pinging back up, like raindrops falling off the eaves of a house into a puddle.

When I was within about twenty feet of the isle, I saw movement to my left. I looked over, and there was J.J.

He grabbed me by the arm, but the rain coming down all around us was so loud I couldn't hear what he was telling me. His fingers dug into my arm, a persistent grip that annoyed me. Dragging me behind him, he turned and began to tread water. I wrenched away, turned around, and quickly swam those last twenty feet. My fingers brushed the grainy surface of the isle.

When I turned to swim back to the beach, I was instantly struck by J.J.'s face. I paused for a moment and watched him. He'd always been a passive and reserved boy, but just then I saw the most intense look I'd ever seen on his face. He stared at me, his lips pressed together, head angled down so that his chin grazed the water. It was like he wasn't J.J. at all. Did he hate me? Or was it anger on his face, an anger that was turning to hatred?

We began to swim back at a frantic pace. At one point, I felt our bodies synchronize, or maybe I just imagined it.

Lightning lit the sky. I felt a wave wash over my head, knocking me under for a moment. I resurfaced, blubbering and spitting out water. About halfway to shore, I looked back to see a larger wave coming at me. That time, I was able to at least hold my breath before I went under.

J.J. pulled himself from the water and turned to look over his shoulder for me. I rode the last wave in and allowed it to wash me ashore. As he ran toward the covered porch, I looked back again. How lucky I was to get back in time. For the most part, we'd been swimming with the current. As I watched the water rising a dozen feet above the little isle, I knew there was no way I could've fought the current and won.

Rain came down steadily. Through the twilight and the sheets of falling water, I could see that Mark was doubled over. Vic knelt in front of him, examining something on his foot.

As I climbed the plank steps under the porch canopy, I heard J.J. ask, "What happened?"

"There was a broken bottle in the sand. He gashed his foot on it," Vic told us.

"Can you walk on it?" J.J. asked.

Mark stood, but as soon as he put weight on the foot, he winced and sat down again. Blood gushed from the cut and onto the porch planks.

J.J. pointed down the beach. "Lena, go run down to Mr. Mason's. Call an ambulance to meet us on the mainland ferry dock. Tell Mason to let us borrow his boat."

I froze for a second, and he said, "Go on! Hurry up, girl!"

I turned, flew down the porch steps, and took off running down the beach. My wet hair was plastered against my face.

I must've made it to Uncle Lonnie's house in about two minutes. I burst through the door, breathless.

"What is it, child?" Lonnie's wife, Karen, asked me.

"Is Uncle Lonnie here? My friend cut his foot on a bottle at the beach. It's gushing blood. We need to ferry him over to the mainland."

She looked down at me. No doubt she'd seen quite a lot of my skin before. I'd worn two-piece swimsuits to the beach since primary school. But my outfit just then—the wet and soggy cotton panties and the faded old push-up bra—was enough to make her pause and frown.

"He down at the store. The keys is on the counter over there. You need me to ride with y'all?"

I grabbed the keys. "I-I don't know. I guess."

She stepped closer and put her hand on mine, took the keys away. "C'mon, child," she said. She snatched up the phone and called the ambulance.

We drove Lonnie's truck down to the beach. When they saw the truck, they hustled up the hill toward us—Vic and J.J. on either side of Mark, who had one arm slung around each of their shoulders for support. His bad foot was raised, and he hopped on his good one. Once J.J. helped him into the back of the truck, Karen drove back to her house and we all loaded into the motorboat. As she steered us through the water, she called out to J.J., "Look in that plastic bag and give him some of that antiseptic spray."

J.J. did as he was told and sprayed Mark's foot with the medicine.

Vic handed me my sundress and sandals. As I slipped them on, I caught J.J.'s eye. He'd been staring at me, but when he caught me looking he turned his attention back to Mark's foot.

The rain had stopped, but the water was still choppy, and it slowed us down. When we got to the ferry dock, an ambulance was already sitting there waiting for us.

Karen told J.J. and Vic to take the boat home. "We'll call Lonnie to pick us up later," she said.

Karen and I rode in back of the ambulance with Mark.

Mark's mama, Mrs. Miller, was in the emergency waiting room. I'd never met her before, yet I knew her as soon as I saw her. She had the same deep-set eyes as Mark, and they each had a tall, lanky body. I couldn't help but worry about her impression of me. She kept looking down at my dress, which was mostly dry, except for the places where my wet underwear dampened it. My sand-encrusted feet and ankles made my skin look dry and gray.

"You don't have to wait here with me," Mrs. Miller said to us. She hoisted her shoulder bag up. "I've got it from here, thank you."

I wondered if Mrs. Miller blamed us for Mark's accident. Would Mark blame us?

Karen touched her shoulder, but Mrs. Miller looked down at Karen's hand with disgust, as though Karen were somehow diseased.

As we exited the emergency room doors, Karen said, "I don't know why it's so important for those uppity folks to like you."

We missed the last ferry, so Karen called Uncle Lonnie to pick us up. We had to walk a good ways back to the dock to meet his boat, and I wanted to talk to Karen about Mark and his mama and about J.J., but I felt too shy to say anything.

When we finally got back to the island, Lonnie offered to drive me home, but I told him I'd rather walk.

The rain had cleared away. The cloudless sky created the perfect backdrop for the white gulls that flew overhead. As I walked past the other island neighborhood, Water Haven, with its porch lights and moss-covered trees, I could see the blue store ahead of me. J.J. worked there after school and on weekends. There was something very comforting about being able to go there and talk with him while he swept floors or stocked shelves. I'd miss that once he moved away.

Inside the blue store, the Mason brothers were playing checkers. They sat on barstools against a wall catty-corner to the register.

"Hey, guhl," they greeted me as I walked in.

J.J. was stocking a cooler with Cokes and juices. I sat down on one of the little stools in front of the register and waited for him to come around. After a few minutes of watching the Mason brothers' checkers game, I looked back to see J.J. just standing there, watching me. He turned back to the cooler and muttered something.

"Just came to tell you the news about Mark. He needed stitches but he'll be fine."

"I figured as much. People don't usually die from a cut on the foot," he said.

I went over and poked him in the ribs.

"Damn it, Lena. Quit it!"

I didn't realize I was back-stepping until my elbow banged against a shelf.

The Mason brothers went silent, watching us. I grinned at them, trying to make light of everything.

Though the cooler was full to bursting with drinks, J.J. stood there with his hand on the door, as though he needed to add more to it. After a moment, I saw that it wasn't the drinks he was looking at. Instead, he used the glass door as a mirror to watch me.

I stared at his back a moment, until I realized he wanted me to leave. He wasn't cruel enough to say it aloud, but I got the message just the same.

"See you later," I said, looking in the direction of the Mason brothers.

"Bye," they said.

The next day, everyone held a farewell party for J.J. He was set to start basic training the following week, and he'd be flying out of Charleston that night.

I didn't go to J.J.'s farewell party. Instead, I watched from my bedroom window seat, hugging a fluffy pillow to my chest.

Through the window, I could see all the well-wishers—Old Miss Mason, back slightly stooped, gave everyone her dimpled, toothless smile; the youngest Mason girl in a dress that kept lifting around her knees as she twirled; and Delia Shackleford, the sweetest woman in the world, who wouldn't let J.J. leave without handing him an envelope full of church money she'd collected for him.

Someone had strung tealights around the porch railing of the blue store, brightening what was already the brightest building on the island. Lonnie and Karen lived two houses down to the right of the store. People moved back and forth between the blue store and Karen's house, the site of the pork barbecue.

I lifted the window halfway, so I could smell everything. Uncle Lonnie Mason made a barbeque sauce with a twinge of garlic and hot pepper. It always tasted sweet and tangy. I could smell that, along with the tender meat that I knew was falling off the bones. That's how they did it on our island. They cooked the pig over charcoals in an open pit. Lonnie and Karen—one or the other, or maybe both—had sat out with the pig all night, swathing it in sauce and turning the bits of flesh over until it grew so tender you could easily break it apart in your hands.

That morning, Granny and Vic had gone over to Karen's to steam crabs and make a peanut stew.

My mouth watered, and I put my nose down to the window screen and breathed in. My stomach moaned for a plate of pulled pork on a bed of Charleston yellow rice.

J.J. cut through our yard on his way out to the blue store. I slid back from the window so he couldn't see me. He stood in our yard, peering at the door, as though waiting for something.

Me?

Then, someone I couldn't see called J.J.'s name. Looking over his shoulder, he called back to them and laughed.

My nine-year-old cousin Damian took my bike off the front porch. I heard the wheels bump against the porch steps as he rolled it down. Then, his little snot-nosed self rode it out toward the blue store.

I sat in the window all afternoon, looking out, and occasionally flipping channels on the TV.

As the light began to dim outside my window, J.J.'s old truck lumbered down the sandy road between my house and Vic's. I knew he was headed out to catch the last ferry.

He halted for a second in front of the house, the engine rumbling as it idled there.

I knew that for the rest of my life I'd never be as comfortable with anyone as I was with Vic and J.J. No one really knows you unless he knew you as a child. A new friend would not have memories of me putting my bloody tooth on his dinner plate, or swimming in synch during a summer storm.

Most of the well-wishers had gone inside the blue store to laugh and tell stories; the others went home, carrying plates of barbecue and seafood and stew. Somehow, I knew this time was meant for J.J. and me. I was supposed to go to him, or maybe he should have come to me. That's how it *should* have been, but neither was to be.

His eyes found my silhouette in the window. He raised a hand in passing. I stared as he pulled onto Ferry Road, and I watched his taillights disappear into the trees.

White Jesus

Janice turned off the main highway and onto a gravel dirt road. My stomach rolled over as the car picked up speed. She took the narrow, twisted road as fast as she could. Dust kicked up from the tires.

"Wanna fly, Lynne?" Janice asked me.

She slammed on the gas pedal. The car zoomed up the hill. I felt it peak, and then the entire Celica lifted off the road. For a moment I felt the sensation of flying, and then we dropped quickly onto all four wheels as we started down the hill. I squealed and laughed out loud.

Janice took her eyes off the road a moment and reached toward the back seat. Two tires skidded off the road and onto the shoulder. "Take the wheel," she said to me.

I reached over and held it steady while she rooted around in the back seat. "Here it is, Lynne," she said, plopping a glossy teen magazine onto my lap. She took the wheel again, and I began to flip through the pages. I found the picture of Antoine Jacoby she'd told me about earlier at school. Antoine is a Black rapper with dark skin and a chiseled face. The picture looked fine, but nothing special. He stood shirtless with his hat turned backward. I liked him, but I wasn't obsessed with him like Janice, who had a thing for Black musicians, the gangster type, which was strange because she was so country, hillbilly even.

Janice is white, and I am Black. Sometimes she commented about us being different races. She asked me why Black girls don't have long hair. Once, when we were eating our school lunches out on the breezeway, she looked over at me and said, "Boy, I love fried chicken. I must have some Black blood in me." She laughed, and her white teeth contrasted with her reddish-brown skin.

When Janice made comments like that, I wondered if she and I could ever become close friends. She confided in me, though I never felt quite comfortable enough to trust her. More than once I'd asked myself, "Is Janice *really* my friend?" There were two other students at the school whom I sometimes wanted to hang out with. Kasha and Richie. They both had the same lunch period as me, and they had a habit of staring, heads tilted down and narrowed eyes filled with dislike (or maybe distrust), as the other kids walked by. Kasha mean-mugged anyone who walked near. Richie, one of the few Hispanic kids at our school, was slightly friendlier than Kasha. They reminded me of the Black and brown kids I'd known back home in New Jersey—poor kids who had strict parents and liked the same R&B music as me.

I flipped past Antoine Jacoby's picture and looked at the rust-colored fall clothes in the magazine. "What time's the church service start?" I asked.

"It's a prayer meeting, not a church service," Janice said, taking her eyes off the road to look over at me. "It's at four." She rolled her eyes. "Don't know why you wore a blame fancy dress."

I always thought it strange that Janice used the word "blame" like a curse word, as in, "Shut your blame mouth. Blame you!"

"Isn't that what you're supposed to wear to church?" I asked.

At my old church in New Jersey, nearly everyone wore dressy clothes. My mom wore wide-brimmed hats to church, like something you'd see on Queen Elizabeth.

Janice loved to tan, but she had loud, red curls and her skin was not supposed to be anything other than white. Once per week after school she'd drive over to the Nail-N-Tan salon by the stoplight in town. Janice said being dark made her clothes look better. I disagreed. Nothing could make the busted outfits she wore look any less odd. Take today for example. Underneath her open cardigan, she wore a T-shirt that said, "Kiss me, I'm Irish." Feather earrings dangled above her shoulders. Her long legs were covered by an ankle-length denim skirt. She wore tennis shoes and thick, white socks.

We were on a long, twisted road with cattle and chicken houses lining the sides. I swear there were more chicken houses than people houses, and boy did it smell. We stayed on the dirt road for about two miles before she finally pulled up to a small, clapboard house with a steeple on top. There were no other houses in sight, just grass in the front yard and dense trees in back. Two tall oak trees hovered over the house. More sunlight would've livened it up.

Janice didn't have air conditioning in her car, so my body was covered in dry sweat. I patted the top of my hair. Luckily, my French braid hadn't come loose in the wind. I'm not a prim-and-proper person, but my mom always tried to guilt me into being one. She got pregnant with me when she was my age, sixteen, and it made her strict, as if she thought that my being sweaty and wild-haired could somehow put a baby in me.

Janice climbed out of the car and darted up the steps, but I hung back. Two jack-o'-lanterns sat on either side of the bottom porch step. Carved pumpkins give me the creeps. Every time I look at one, I remember how slimy its insides feel.

The glass doors led into a foyer with cats lounging around inside it. Their fluffy hair and long tails moved back and forth in front of the glass door. Cats may be even worse than carved pumpkins. At least pumpkins don't stalk you or unnerve you with neon-colored eyes. Janice held open the front door for me, and when she realized I wasn't on her heels, she asked, "What's wrong?"

She stood at the top of the steps looking down at me. When I was about halfway up the steps, she yawned and stretched her arms wide. The sweater fanned out below her arms; she looked like a black crow with its wings spread.

I exhaled, relaxed my shoulders, and followed her inside the foyer, where the cats rubbed their coats against our legs. Janice picked one up and kissed its nose.

We entered the meeting hall and Janice put the cat down on a pew, and then she went over and threw her arms around a robed woman. They hugged a moment, and when Janice pulled away she said, "This is Lynne, my friend from school, Mama."

Mrs. Munson was tall like Janice but appeared taller due to her upright posture. On a shorter woman, the long, black minister's robe would have dragged the floor, but not on Mrs. Munson, who gave me a little wave and turned back to the flock of women gathered around her. Others stood in line to shake her hand. A few people milled around the room or sat in the pews. Most were older, in their fifties and sixties.

I took a seat in one of the pews toward the back. People kept smiling at me and coming over to shake hands. The whole congregation was white, except for one old Black woman and a little boy I guessed was her grandson.

After a while, Janice's mom led us all in prayer. Then, she released us so that we could kneel and say our own prayers. I eased myself back onto the wooden pew and watched everyone else pray until Pastor Munson announced the call to worship. She came down from the pulpit. We all stood as she opened the doors of the church, inviting us to come forward with sin.

A young man with too-long hair walked up the aisle.

Several members of the congregation clapped and squealed, "Hallelujah!" and "Praise Him!"

"I need God now because I want to accept His will and His way," the man began. He took a deep breath and then added, "I've backslid and fallen into drinking. I've cheated on my wife, Kate."

I glanced over my shoulder at where he'd walked from. A woman Janice had been talking to earlier, the one with the upswept hairdo, stood red-faced, holding a baby in her arms. She must've been his wife, Kate. A child of about three years old stood beside Kate and the baby. I would've been ashamed, but Kate just stood there stone-faced, bouncing the baby on her hip.

After the last "Amen," we all went down to the fellowship hall for dinner. Platters of country ham, mac and cheese, and corn muffins lay out on the counter. Janice fluttered around the room like a butterfly, laughing and talking with everyone. Though they were all friendly, I felt uncomfortable and worried I'd say the wrong thing. I was not a Christian and had never been, despite all those hours in church with my family when I was little. I occasionally took the Lord's name in vain and didn't even read the scriptures. These people, of course, wouldn't like that. They wouldn't like *me.*

I told Janice I'd meet her out at the Celica. As I sat in the car eating my dinner, a teenage boy shot hoops on a blacktop at the edge of the church parking lot. He dribbled the ball a couple of times, then sprang up and shot the ball into the basket. Once he'd made a few shots in a row, he walked to the edge of a small cliff, pulled himself up on his tiptoes, and balanced right at the lip of the drop-off. The sun was nearly gone, and the sky had become a mix of purple and pink. The incline wasn't too steep, but there was probably a twenty-foot drop below him.

"Come away from there," I whispered.

Just when I thought he'd for sure lose his balance, he stepped back, grabbed his ball, and walked away, his footsteps crunching on the gravel.

Before long, most of the other cars in the lot were gone. Janice leaned out of the side door and motioned for me. "Come help me," she said.

In the church kitchen, the sink was piled high with dirty dishes. She picked up a dish towel and tossed it at me. "I'll wash and you dry," she said. Janice squirted green Palmolive all over the dishes and turned on the faucet. She let the water run. Steam floated above the plates, the plastic tumblers, and the shiny glasses.

"I'm glad I invited you here, Lynne," she said and leaned closer to me as if to reveal a secret. "I didn't tell Mama you were Black. Wasn't sure she'd let you visit with us."

"*What?*"

"She just don't approve of Blacks and whites together," Janice said, like it was no big deal. "And she's very religious, don't believe in a lot of things, probably 'cause she's wanting to be a pastor."

I shook my head. "This isn't even a real church. You have cats all over the place, and your mom didn't even read from scripture."

"She wasn't *supposed* to read from scripture. It was a prayer meeting." She sucked in her breath and put her palms against the lip of the sink. "Look, Lynne. Please don't be mad at me. You're still my best friend. It's just that folks like my mama don't believe Blacks and whites should mix, that's all."

"Then why the hell am I here?! Why'd you invite me?"

"Well, Mama don't think Blacks and whites should marry or anything like that, but it's okay for me to be friends with them." She stacked three plates in front of me. "You're my friend, Lynne. Mama knows that. She don't care that you're Black, as long as you ain't a guy."

"So if I were a guy, you couldn't hang around me?"

"You *ain't* a guy." She dipped her hands into the sink and coated them with poofs of tiny bubbles. She flicked the bubbles at me.

"Quit it," I said, and dropped the towel on top of the wet plates.

My own mother had sat me down long before we'd come to Muscadine and told me that some people might say racist things to me. These comments were not my fault, Mom had said, and I shouldn't feel bad. The problem was that I *did* feel bad. Had I done something to not deserve Janice's friendship? And if so many kids in my class made fun of Black speech or said things like "She's pretty for a Black girl," then there must be some truth in their statements, right? I shook my head, fighting to clear those thoughts away.

"You're going to take me home," I said, turning toward the door.

"Nooo," she said in a long, slow breath. When my family had first moved to Georgia, I admired the women's drawls. Waitresses in restaurants let syllables drip from their lips like honey, but Janice's accent didn't sound charming just then. It was a pathetic twang.

"Lynne," she said. "It's nearly dark. I ain't driving you back right now. I'll take you back on Sunday, just like we planned it."

I grabbed my purse from the bench by the wall and started up the basement stairs. By the time I reached the top, she'd come up behind me and grabbed my elbow. "Please, Lynne," she said. "I'm sorry about the Black stuff. We're still friends, okay?" She took my bag from me.

I knew Janice felt as lonely as I did. I was the new kid in a mostly white school, and she was so strangely religious and not wealthy enough or popular enough to get invited to most of the parties. Still, no matter how lonely I was, I didn't want to stay.

"Give me my bag," I said, trying to snatch it away. She held it over her head. Because I was several inches shorter, I couldn't quite reach it. She grinned down at me in the way older kids smirk at younger ones for being afraid of the dark.

"Give it to me," I said, embarrassed at how whiny my voice sounded.

I reached for the bag again and tried to push her up against the wall with my shoulder, but she ducked around me. I was at the top step when I lost my balance, felt my body go into freefall. The moment seemed to last longer than it did. How long could it take to fall down a flight of stairs?

Janice screamed as I tried to catch hold of the handrail. My fingers scratched the wall. Bits of the plaster tore loose and stuck beneath my nails. Luckily, my flailing slowed the fall, and I landed on my butt at the bottom of the staircase.

My thumbnail had snapped down to the quick; blood seeped from under the nail and mixed with the red nail polish. I glanced up the stairs and saw that I'd left scratch marks on the wall in two or three places. She helped me to my feet, and I rubbed my sore behind. A sharp pain radiated from my right elbow and up toward my shoulder. I must've bumped my arm against the wall.

"Are you okay?" Janice asked. "It's all my fault. If I hadn't pulled away like that . . ." she said. Tears welled in her eyes. "We gotta git you to a hospital." She looked around frantically. "Where're my dang keys?"

"No," I said. "I'll be fine. My butt's just sore, and my fingernails."

"Thank God you didn't bang your head on the floor. You coulda been really hurt," Janice said. "I'll get you some Band-Aids for your fingers." She stepped over and opened a door beneath the staircase. Janice brought me a bottle of rubbing alcohol, cotton balls, and Band-Aids. In the kitchen, I cleaned and bandaged my fingers.

Janice's mother came down the stairs and Janice went back to work, helping her mom put the kitchen to rights. I immediately felt betrayed as I watched Janice smile up at her mother, a woman who didn't like me and didn't want me there. Couldn't Janice at least *try* to be on my side? I hadn't done anything to her mother, and I didn't deserve to be looked down on. Mrs. Munson wasn't outright rude to me, but she didn't look at me. Not at all. It was like I wasn't there. My own mother had warned me about people like her, but I'd dismissed her comments as paranoid.

Janice took her time cleaning the kitchen, and I waited for her in the car. I didn't have to ask again for her to take me home. Moonlight glinted off the Indian-head coin on my bracelet as we passed the lights heading back toward my house in town. I thought of flying in the Celica, hovering in midair. Freefalling down the stairs. I remembered the boy who had played basketball near the hill and how he didn't seem afraid of falling. Why hadn't he been more fearful that he'd be hurt? Maybe he knew the feeling of freefall and wanted to feel it again.

On Monday, Janice waved at me in the hallway, but I avoided eye contact and moved purposefully to the outside lunch tables.

It was homecoming week, and students were encouraged to dress in themed costumes. That day was Senior Citizens' Day, so most of the kids wore old-fashioned clothes and glasses. Some carried canes. One or two even moved around in wheelchairs. From my spot near the grass, I overheard Kasha and Richie talking behind me. Kasha was dissing other students' outfits as Richie braided her hair.

Richie gave me a nod and smiled at me, and I got up and carried my lunch tray over to them. He had light brown skin and curly black hair. Richie wore every shade in a box of crayons, and he wore everything at once: half a dozen bangle bracelets, multiple pairs of earrings, and streaks of pink synthetics braided into his hair (even though the principal had threatened him with a suspension already).

I sat with them for the rest of homecoming week. A few times I looked up to see Janice standing on the other side of the glass door, watching us. Each day, Richie spent half the lunch period combing my hair. He'd practice French braiding or cornrowing while Kasha went off about our classmates. She hated the girls on the homecoming court simply because they were on the court and moved so self-assuredly. When they entered a room, people shouted their names. Kasha had the same hatred for a handful of guys at our school, guys who got slapped on the back or were smiled at much more often than everyone else. Richie and Kasha had learned that they couldn't be self-assured. To act self-assured when you were someone like Richie would end in being slapped back with slurs and curses. Even though Kasha was on the basketball team, she wasn't one of the stars. She'd barely played in any of the ball games, and I think she envied girls like Lucy Boudreaux. Kasha had friends, but she still seemed unhappy most of the time.

Richie had a big truck, just like the redneck boys, and the three of us rode around in it on homecoming Friday. We parked on a country road and talked, pretending to not be curious about what was happening at the stadium. Though we were miles out, sound carried through those hills, and we heard the drums banging away during the halftime show. We sat on the back of Richie's truck and shared a cigar Richie had stolen from his grandfather. I didn't like the nutty taste of the cigar, but the smoke caused a warming sensation in my nose, which I liked, and I loved the sweet, smoky smell.

"Did your friend Janice go to homecoming?" Kasha asked, smiling bitchy at me. Kasha had seen Janice watching me through the glass door at lunch a few times, and for whatever reason she liked to tease me about it.

"Why aren't you there now dancing with your boyfriend D.W.?" I said. Usually, I didn't bite back at Kasha, but I'd had enough of her. I knew that she and D.W. had broken up and I wanted to rub her nose in it.

Richie sucked in his breath, obviously surprised by my comeback.

There was a full moon that night and Richie had left his truck's headlights on, but I still struggled to see anything more than a few feet in front of me. I could see Kasha's face, though, and she was beautiful—one of those Black girls who had skin so clear it looked unreal. If only she weren't so catty and sarcastic, maybe I could connect with her like I did with Richie.

I said, "You know I'm not her friend. I just went to church with her that one time."

My words sounded unconvincing, even to myself. I wanted to put as much distance between Janice Munson and me as possible. No way I would admit to Kasha that I sat back and let Janice make those racist jokes and comments to me. What would Kasha have done? She probably would've smacked Janice or at least cursed her to hell and back.

Kasha let out a laugh. "What religion is she? Holiness?"

It took me a moment to answer her. She surprised me by not staying angry at my D.W. comment. Then I realized the secret to gaining Kasha's approval: *Don't let her run over you; stick up for yourself.*

"Nondenominational," I answered, my response sounding like a question. I didn't know what nondenominational meant.

Kasha took the cigar from Richie and brought it to her lips. Smoke billowed out toward me. "We should go to it," she said.

"The church?" I asked. "I'm not even sure how to get there."

"We can find it," Richie said. He loved to drive anywhere and everywhere.

After a half hour of taking side streets and dirt roads, we wound up in the parking lot of the little clapboard house with the steeple on top, Richie's headlights throwing light across the front entrance.

"Are those the steps she pushed you down?" Kasha asked, nodding toward the porch.

"No," I said. "She didn't—"

Kasha opened the passenger door and climbed down from the truck. Richie got out then, too, and I followed. Kasha tried the front entrance, but it was locked, of course. Richie said he had a screwdriver, and I watched as he ran back down the steps to get it. Using Richie's tool, Kasha pried the door open, and we followed her into the foyer. The old saying "quiet as a church" ran through my head as we entered the sanctuary. The headlights from Richie's truck cast a strange light into the room. Though the beams were mostly blocked by the front wall of the church, slants of light came in through the two front windows, casting shadows on the pews and the lectern.

Kasha ran ahead of us and down the aisle to the pulpit, where she climbed up to the preacher's lectern and banged her hand on it. Her voice thundered out words like *sinners* and *god damn you!* Richie sat down on a pew in the back, and the smoke from his cigar began to waft around the room. I walked up and down an outside aisle, running my fingers over the cold wood of each pew as I passed it.

There, on the wall, was a picture of Jesus, his eyes raised heavenward, as if in prayer, though I detected a hint of condescension in those eyes, that same condescension Janice had shown while washing dishes with me. Smug Jesus suddenly irritated all hell out of me with his long, hillbilly hair and pale skin. Something festered inside me, and I didn't realize how much until I had reached up, pulled white Jesus from the wall, and brought his image down over the back of one of the pews. The painting didn't break from the first blow, but I could feel the frame bend. I hit it again, and then a third time. By then, Richie had come over and was standing a safe distance away from me, watching. Kasha had grown silent up in the pulpit. It was strange to think I'd been worried about coming in here, worried that they might steal something or vandalize the place.

Once I'd finished smashing the painting all to hell, Richie took my hand and walked the three of us out. As we pulled away from the clapboard, whitewashed building, I imagined Janice's mother coming in to find the lock broken, the door ajar, and Jesus's white face in ruins, broken into so many pieces she'd never be able to put them back together.

Acknowledgments

Dozens of people have helped me develop on the way to publication. Thanks to Alice Friman, Allen Gee, Martin Lammon, Laura Newbern, Peter Selgin, and all my workshop classmates at Georgia College. Thanks to all the teachers, writers, and fellow students I studied with at University of Southern Mississippi, but especially to Steven Barthelme, Anne Sanow, Angela Ball, Martina Sciolino, and Sherita Johnson, who read and commented on early drafts of several of these stories.

I've also been fortunate enough to publish the following stories in the following journals: "You Can Have It" (formerly called "Tim") in *Still: The Journal;* "Kasha and Ansley" in *storySouth,* "June's Menorah" in *Big Muddy;* "Black Water" in *Southeast Review;* "Gullah Babies" in *South Carolina Review;* "The Sense of Touch" in *Oxford American;* "Gris-Gris" in *Good River Review;* and "The Daughter" in the anthology *Stories That Need to Be Told,* edited by Jennifer Top. Thanks to the staff and editors of all those wonderful publications.

I've also benefited from the encouragement of my colleagues at Tennessee Tech University, particularly Ted Pelton, Andrew Smith, Scott Stenson, and Erin Hoover, who care about the craft and the power of writing. Thank you to Denton Loving for giving me time and a place to write at the Orchard Keeper Writers' Residency. I'd also like to thank my current writing group members: Martha Highers, Phyllis

Brotherton, and Miriam Levi. Thanks also to everyone associated with *Under the Sun,* a lovely magazine that has helped me sharpen my editorial skills.

I owe a huge thanks to Silas House, my editor, who helped me improve these stories and gave me so much guidance to create a book of which I'm proud. I want to thank everyone at the University Press of Kentucky, especially Patrick O'Dowd and Erin Holman, who were so supportive and helpful. I am also grateful to the cover designer, Kathleen Lynch, for this lovely cover.

I owe a big thank-you to my mother, Annie Lee, who donated all those free babysitting hours while I worked on these stories. And thanks to my son, Andrew, who inspires me without even trying.